UNDER SURVEILLANCE

GAYLE WILSON

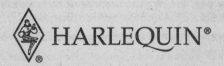

HARLEQUIN®

TORONTO • NEW YORK • LONDON
AMSTERDAM • PARIS • SYDNEY • HAMBURG
STOCKHOLM • ATHENS • TOKYO • MILAN • MADRID
PRAGUE • WARSAW • BUDAPEST • AUCKLAND

ISBN 0-373-22743-4

UNDER SURVEILLANCE

ABOUT THE AUTHOR

Five-time RITA® Award finalist and RITA® Award winner Gayle Wilson has written twenty-seven novels and two novellas for Harlequin/Silhouette. She has won more than forty awards and nominations for her work.

Gayle still lives in Alabama, where she was born, with her husband of thirty-three years. She loves to hear from readers. Write to her at P.O. Box 3277, Hueytown, AL 35023. Visit Gayle online at http://suspense.net/gayle-wilson.

Books by Gayle Wilson

Don't miss any of our special offers. Write to us at the following address for information on our newest releases.

Harlequin Reader Service
U.S.: 3010 Walden Ave., P.O. Box 1325, Buffalo, NY 14269
Canadian: P.O. Box 609, Fort Erie, Ont. L2A 5X3

FOR YOUR EYES ONLY

NSA
AGENT PROFILE

NAME: JOHN EDMONDS
DATE OF BIRTH: SEPTEMBER 27, 1965
ASSIGNED TEAM: CLASSIFIED

SPECIAL SKILLS: Hand-to-hand combat; expert
                     marksman; cryptanalyst; skilled
                     in intelligence analysis; electronic
                     warfare expert.

AGENT EVALUATION: Independent, determined and
                     highly motivated. Capable of
                     thinking outside the box.

STATUS: Retired from government
                     service

CURRENT ADDRESS: The Phoenix Brotherhood

FOR YOUR EYES ONLY

CAST OF CHARACTERS

Kelly Lockett—She had inherited the charitable foundation her dead brother had founded. The only trouble was she had inherited his enemies, as well.

John Edmonds—A former NSA agent, the Phoenix newcomer had wanted a real case, something he could get his teeth into. He hadn't been prepared for the high society lady who went with it.

Griff Cabot—Griff never expected the minor assignment he'd given the one Phoenix agent he doubted to rock the foundations of Washington and possibly the country.

Catherine Suttle—The ultimate Beltway insider, Catherine knew everybody in D.C. who mattered. Did she hold the key that would unravel the mystery of the secret organization known as The Covenant?

Bertha Reynolds—She had warned Chad Lockett that the charitable foundation he'd built was in trouble, but he hadn't seemed interested. Had that misjudgment cost him his life?

Mark Daniels—Cast into the role of big brother by Chad's death, Mark wanted a very different relationship with Kelly. How far was he willing to go to arrange that?

Hugh Donaldson—No one knew more about the dealings of the Legacy than its chief financial officer. The real question was what else he might know.

Leon Clements—The black sheep of a prominent Maryland family, Leon nursed a deep-seated bitterness that might have driven him to desperate measures.

Trevor Holcomb—He had been responsible for the failed security arrangements on the night of the Legacy Auction. Poor planning, or an attempt to carry out a secret agenda?

For Mollie, my son's wife and the daughter of my heart.

Prologue

t had gotten cramped being in Griff Cabot's doghouse. And it would come as no surprise to anyone who knew him hat John Edmonds didn't like being there.

"More surveillance," he said.

It had not been a question, but the man across the desk aised his head, leveling a pair of remarkably piercing eyes t him. "It is your area of expertise," Griff said.

"Among others."

John was careful to keep any hint of anger from his oice. He *had* worked for the National Security Agency for everal years, but Cabot was well aware of the other skills e'd brought to this organization. And they both understood vhy he wasn't being allowed to use them.

"Surveillance is the one that's needed on this."

Griff's gaze fell back to the paperwork he had been in he process of completing. Perhaps because of his previous osition as assistant deputy director of the CIA, Cabot kept neticulous records. Each of his operatives was still extenvely debriefed at the end of a mission.

Actually, although the Phoenix was a private concern, it inctioned very much like the old External Security Team riff had run at the agency. John had not been a member of that team, and he'd often wondered if that was part of the problem.

As soon as he'd heard about the work the Phoenix was doing, he had approached Cabot with a request to join. In the beginning he had been utilized on a variety of the wide-ranging cases the group undertook. After he'd helped Elizabeth Richards escape, however, that had no longer been true.

He had clearly understood that he was going against Griff's wishes when he'd done that. He had felt, however, that helping Elizabeth reach Rafe Sinclair was important enough that he was willing to take whatever punishment his action would bring. He had just never imagined that chastisement would go on this long.

"Any idea how soon I'll again be allowed to do something *beyond* surveillance?"

Cabot's eyes lifted once more, regarding him steadily, but the head of the Phoenix didn't answer.

"If you want me to quit, Griff," John said, meeting that cold stare, "just say so."

"I'm not trying to run you off."

"Then forgive me for being dense, but what the hell *are* you trying to do?"

Griff's lips pursed. When he opened them, he said exactly what John had expected. "I'm trying to determine if you're capable of following orders. Especially those you don't like."

"If I hadn't helped Elizabeth, Rafe would be dead," John said patiently. "Would you have preferred that?"

"You believe the end justifies the means."

"In that situation. Rafe was operating under a handicap no one was aware of. You had given him your word that you wouldn't interfere. I'd made no such promise. Elizabeth's argument that Rafe shouldn't face that kind of danger alone made sense to me. In the end—''

"The salient point," Cabot interrupted, "is that I'd given my word the Phoenix wouldn't interfere. It was what Rafe wanted. I'd vowed to honor his wish in exchange for his undertaking a job no one else could have done. You were aware of what I'd promised on behalf of the Phoenix, and yet you chose to disregard it."

Which was all true, as far as it went. In John's opinion it didn't go nearly far enough.

"This isn't personal, believe me," Griff went on after a few seconds of awkward silence. "I'm responsible for the people who work for me. I have to know that when I send out an operative, he'll follow orders."

"You hadn't given me any orders. Not concerning Elizabeth."

"Which is the only reason you're still here. I gave you the benefit of the doubt. I won't do it again. If you no longer wish to participate in the Phoenix under those conditions, I'll understand."

John had been tempted to resign more than once during these past few difficult months. Openly faced with that choice at last, he realized he wasn't ready to give up.

And if he weren't, he knew his only option was to ride out Griff's displeasure. Even in the short time he'd known Rafe Sinclair, he had come to the conclusion that helping save the former agent's life was worth whatever it cost him personally.

Besides, he believed in the organization Griff, Hawk, and Jordan Cross had created four years ago. The Phoenix was a private agency designed to use the formidable skills Griff's former CIA antiterrorism team possessed to obtain justice for those who couldn't find it any other way.

"I'm not ready to quit," he said, meeting Cabot's eyes.

After another moment of silence, Cabot searched through the stack of manila folders on the corner of his desk. He extracted one and slid it across a vastness of well-polished mahogany.

"Surveillance, but not exactly the type you've been doing. Maybe this will be more to your liking," Griff said, tilting his head in the direction of the folder that lay between them.

"What is it?"

John deliberately left the file lying unopened. He had always learned more from Cabot's sound bites than from his own first reading of a file. He waited for this one, tamping down the excitement Griff's brief description had already created.

Surveillance, but not exactly the type you've been doing. In his opinion, anything that wasn't what he had been doing would be an improvement.

"Something that caused a blip on Ethan Snow's mental radar during his last assignment. A name that showed up where it shouldn't. All you have to do is some discreet nosing around. *Very* discreet. I don't want to set off alarms anywhere. This is a highly respected organization."

For a second John thought Cabot meant the Phoenix. It was unlikely that reference was to the agency, however, since most of their clients learned of them through the same kind of discreet word-of-mouth Griff had just alluded to. And if not the Phoenix…

He reached out, pulling the folder toward him. When he opened it, the heading at the top, in Snow's neat handwriting, was enough to let him know Cabot's warning had been an understatement. His low whistle was an unthinking reaction to how respected the organization this file referred to actually was.

"Exactly," Griff said. "You *do* have a tux, I assume."

He didn't, but he wasn't going to admit that to Cabot, who probably owned a dozen.

"Of course," John lied, wondering how quickly he could have one fitted.

"Then I suggest you start with the enclosed invitation."

John slipped the heavy cream rectangle out of its envelope, quickly reading the information embossed on the front.

"It's quite legitimate, I assure you. And rather costly," Cabot added, and he should know. His background was exactly the kind of silver spoon stuff that would get someone invited to those kinds of events. "It will allow you a foot in the door. Strictly for observation, of course."

"Once I'm in, what exactly am I looking for?"

"I'm not sure. What caused Ethan's concern is outlined in the file. As I said, this may be nothing, but I've learned to trust the instincts of my people through the years, especially those of someone like Ethan. If something about that group caused him concern, that's reason enough for me to want them checked out. Besides, the food is usually superb."

If someone as wealthy as Griff considered the dinner to be "costly," then it damn well *should* be good, John thought.

"Oh, and there's an auction," Griff added as John rose, holding onto the file he'd been given, "so watch your body language. I'm not sure we have enough in the budget to cover any unexpected purchases."

"What's on the block?"

"Celebrity dresses, I believe. You should be safe there," Cabot went on dryly, his eyes falling once more to the paperwork before him. "I doubt they'll have anything in your color."

Chapter One

Although Kelly Lockett knew to the last person how many patrons crowded the ballroom of the downtown hotel, she could see almost none of them. Their faces were lost in the darkness beyond the glare of the spotlights directed at the podium. She waited a moment for the applause to die down before she lifted her hand, gesturing for silence as if she had been doing this her entire life.

Actually, she had avoided such functions like the plague. They were the kind of thing Chad loved, so she had always let him handle them. Thankfully, he had turned out to be incredibly good at it.

So good that she couldn't hope to fill his shoes, she thought with a swell of anxiety. Then she reminded herself that trying to take her brother's place wasn't why she was here.

"On behalf of my brother," she began, speaking over the remaining splatters of applause.

Before she had gotten the last word out of her mouth, the clapping began again, growing into a thunderous ovation. First the men in their tuxedos and then their elegantly gowned companions began to stand all over the huge room.

Her eyes stung at the strength and duration of their spontaneous tribute. She bit the inside of her bottom lip, determined to get through this evening without crying. So far, all her tears had been shed in private. She didn't intend to make a public spectacle of her grief tonight.

She waited, not attempting to speak until the noise had died down again and the only sounds in the vast ballroom were of people settling back into their chairs. Her eyes had apparently adjusted to the dazzle of light because she could identify some of those seated at the nearest of the small, round tables. Their faces were turned expectantly up to the dais where she stood.

She had made a point of speaking to most of them before dinner, and as much as she dreaded it, she would mingle with the crowd again after the auction. That was another talent Chad had had. Making people feel welcome. Making them want to participate and to feel good about what they were doing.

"Thank you," she said sincerely. Whatever her own motives were for being here tonight, her brother certainly deserved their applause. "As I had started to say, on behalf of my brother, I would like to welcome you to the eighth annual Lockett Legacy Dinner and Auction. As you know, Chad was a tireless fund-raiser for a number of causes, as well as being a true philanthropist himself. This particular event, however, always held a very special place in his heart.

"For one thing, this is the only one of the many organizations to which he devoted his time and considerable energy that bears our family name. For another, the charities to which you have so generously donated each year were chosen by him personally. This foundation was Chad's baby, and I thank you all for continuing the good works he believed in so much."

There was another round of applause, this one more perfunctory than the last. That was all right. The first had been for her brother himself, from his friends and colleagues. To Kelly it had been the far more important response.

"As you know, this year we have a very special auction arranged for you. This, too, was Chad's brainchild, and he worked tirelessly to acquire the items you see around the room." She paused a moment, allowing the audience to focus once more on the glass display cases that lined the walls. "I know he would want me to again thank the donors for making these beautiful garments available, and I do. I should also remind you that because we want to raise as much money as we can tonight, we have accepted a few prebids from some very serious collectors. You'll have plenty of opportunity, I promise, to open your checkbooks and outbid them for anything that catches your eye."

Polite laughter followed the remark, just as the citation in parenthesis on her note cards had said it would. No one who had seen them expected those prebids to be overruled. They had been allowed only on the rarest and most valuable items of tonight's collection, and they had come in from all over the world. Kelly, along with everyone else associated with the Legacy, had been pleasantly surprised at the amounts.

"I rather fancied the off-the-shoulder black dress that belonged to Princess Diana," she continued, following the script she'd been given. "I even thought about breaking open my piggy bank to see if there was enough there to make a down payment."

More polite laughter at what could only be classified as a very lame joke, given the Lockett wealth. And that, too, was okay, Kelly decided.

She had been able to relax a little as she mouthed this nonsense, and the urge to cry for how much better Chad would have done this had finally passed. All she had to do now was give the last of her professionally written introduction, and then the actual auction would begin.

Once it had, she would have a chance to catch her breath. Maybe even to grab a glass of the champagne that would be flowing freely as an inducement to bidding. There was only this one last hurdle to get past.

"Unfortunately, that one didn't fit. A height issue," she said. More laughter at her acknowledgement of her small statue. "Actually, since no alterations were allowed to any of the garments, the dresses our models will wear tonight are recreations of the originals you see in the cases. As is this."

She stepped from behind the lectern and walked to the head of the raised runway that had been set up in the center of the room. She paused a moment, more to calm her nerves than to showcase the dress, although it surely deserved the spotlight.

Even though she was far more at home in jeans and a sweater, Kelly had to admit there had been something completely sensuous about slipping the flame-red evening gown over her head. With a whisper of silk, it had settled around her hips and breasts like a glove.

Behind her, the voice of the professional announcer picked up where she had left off. "As any couturier will tell you, in order to truly understand the magic of a garment, it is necessary to see it worn. Therefore, we've arranged a very special showing for you tonight."

Carefully coached in the same glide the professional models would use, Kelly began her journey down the runway. The chorus of oohs that followed her was proof that her advisors had been right about the gown. Both the color and its strapless design made it a showstopper. Or in this case, a show starter.

"Miss Lockett is modeling a copy of a vintage Givenchy

with matching stole. The dress was created for Audrey Hepburn, the designer's favorite star, to wear in the film *Funny Face*. I'm sure you all remember the scene in which Miss Hepburn descends the stairs at the Louvre wearing this same gown.''

According to the script, at that exact moment Kelly should have reached the end of the runway, which jutted out into the middle of the room. In front of her was a series of six steps that led down to the floor of the ballroom. Just as Hepburn had in the movie, she raised her arms to shoulder height, displaying the matching red silk stole, before she started down the steps.

''I'll tell you in confidence that there isn't a single prebid on this one,'' the smooth voice from the stage behind her went on. ''We've saved it just for you.''

Kelly had been advised to pick out a couple of people in the crowd to smile or nod to as she descended. She had begun searching the faces around her, looking for a familiar one, when her gaze seemed to lock on a masculine profile. Its features, silhouetted against the lights from the back of the room, were clean and strong, as classically proportioned as if they had been graven on some ancient coin.

At that exact moment, the man turned his head, his eyes meeting and holding hers. She couldn't have said what color they were. Or even what he looked like. All she knew was that he was dark—both eyes and hair. Handsome in a rugged, completely masculine kind of way. Compelling.

Obviously, she thought, relieved when her stride carried her past the table where he was sitting. Although she continued along the predestined route all the models would take, designed to let the guests have a closer look at the garments, she had to resist the urge to turn her head and glance back at him over her shoulder.

And that was totally out of character. Especially given

what had been happening in her life during the last few months.

Finally, thankfully, she reached the end of her performance. Before her were the double doors that led out of the ballroom and back to anonymity, with which she was far more comfortable.

Behind her she heard the auctioneer open the bidding on the original of the Givenchy knock-off she was wearing. The next couple of hours would be someone else's responsibility—his and the other professionals hired from one of the top New York fashion houses. And she was more than ready to hand it over.

As she met the eyes of the security guard at the door, he nodded to her. The gesture somehow reminded her of her strange reaction to the man seated at the foot of the runway steps.

Again she had to force herself not to turn around and search the crowd for him. Of course, it wouldn't matter if she did. All she would be able to see from here was that same sea of people she had faced before. She wouldn't be able to pick him out. And if she encountered him again…

She wouldn't be able to recognize him, she told herself resolutely. What had just occurred had been one of those bizarre incidents that happen to everyone at one time or another. Meeting the eyes of the handsome man in the cab next to you while you waited for a red light. Or in an elevator. Or a restaurant. It was absolutely nothing of consequence.

Which was good, she thought, as she slipped through the doors and out into the hall. She couldn't afford any distractions. Certainly not one as time-consuming as a man like that might prove to be.

IN THE END it was after two o'clock before Kelly managed her escape, slipping out of the ballroom by a back door.

Chad would have teased that that was the story of her life, she acknowledged, as she stood watching the numbers flash by on the parking-deck elevator, but she refused to feel guilty. Most of the crowd had gone. She had done her duty. Paid her dues. Made nice to anyone with a checkbook. Now she was going home.

She hadn't bothered to change out of the copy of the Givenchy she'd modeled. She would return it later.

The elevator doors opened and she stepped out, pulling the red stole more closely around her shoulders. After the heat of the ballroom, the night air felt cool against her skin.

She was surprised to find there were only a handful of cars left on this level. Of course, it had been reserved for those who would come early and leave late. And it seemed that despite her remorse at slipping out early, she must be one of the last to depart.

She started across the concrete, the sound of her high-heeled sandals echoing off steel beams and cement pillars. She expected the security guard to step out of his booth in response to the noise. He didn't, however, and as she came closer to the location, she could tell that the security box was empty.

She glanced at her watch, but it was too dark to see the hands. Maybe security had gone off duty. That was something she should probably mention to the board when they met to rehash tonight's successes and failures. Their patrons had a right to protection, no matter how late they stayed.

Her car, which was actually Chad's car, was parked halfway up the far ramp. Before she headed over to it, she bent her head a little to take another look into the security booth. Definitely empty.

She stopped at the bottom of the ramp. Putting one hand on the cold metal of its railing for balance, she bent her knee, pulling the strap of her sandal more securely onto her heel.

She resisted the temptation to slip the shoes off. Despite the fact that they consisted of only a couple of crossed pieces of leather, by now the sandals had begun to rub. She could imagine what walking barefoot over the rough concrete of the ramp would do to her feet, however.

She looked up to estimate the distance to her car and caught a glimpse of what appeared to be a shadow moving behind or under it. *A rat? Or one of the city's feral cats?* There were plenty of both in D.C., but despite her attempt to find some rational, nonthreatening explanation for what she had just seen, the hair on the back of her neck began to lift, sending a shiver down her spine.

She looked again toward the security booth, an oasis of light in the dimness of the concrete structure, and then once more toward her car. The darkness increased sharply near the top of the ramp where it was parked.

Back to the elevator, she decided without any further hesitation. This time she would do what she should have done in the first place. She would get someone to walk her out here. Whatever was waiting in the shadows up there, she wasn't about to face it on her own.

She turned, already taking the first step in retracing her journey, when her blood froze. Lined up between her and the elevator doors were three men. Or rather three teenagers, she amended, as her eyes skated back and forth between them.

Their youth wasn't comforting. Not given their dress and demeanor. Actually, the latter was distinctly menacing.

As if in response to some unseen signal, they began to walk toward her. All the survival reflexes kicked in, sending a rush of adrenaline through her system.

Fight or flight. A hell of a choice, given that the three of them were blocking the only viable exit.

Maybe she was wrong about what she'd seen behind her car, she thought. Maybe it *had* been a rat. Something other than a cohort of the teens who were now advancing on her.

She slipped the strap of her evening bag off her wrist and fumbled her car keys out of it. Then she threw the purse underhanded toward the trio. It skidded to a stop about ten feet in front of them.

If their intent were to rob her, she'd make it easy for them. Maybe the purse would give them something to occupy themselves with while she made a run up the ramp to the car.

And if another one were waiting for her there, she'd deal with that when she arrived. Those odds were still better than trying to go through these three to get to the elevator.

She thought briefly again about taking off her shoes, but the boys were advancing more quickly now. The bag she'd thrown lay halfway between them and her position.

She had no idea whether they would be sufficiently distracted by it to allow her to escape. That would probably depend on what they wanted. If she tried to run before they had gotten to it, however, they might very well ignore the purse in order to come after her.

Almost before the thought had time to form, the boy in the middle reached the evening bag. He stooped to pick it up, his eyes never leaving hers.

As she watched, he took her wallet out and opened it. He made a show of running his thumb across the money in the bill compartment. She couldn't remember how much was there. She never carried much cash, so it couldn't be a great deal.

Please, God, let it be enough.

Then, without bothering to remove the money, he threw

both the purse and billfold to the side and took another step toward her. As soon as he did, she rounded the railing, sprinting up the ramp toward her brother's Jag.

The sound of their boots, amplified by the low overhang, pounded against the concrete behind her. She could tell that they were gaining on her. She released the stole she had unthinkingly hung on to and used both hands to pick up the long skirt of the red dress, freeing her legs from its constraints.

As she neared her car, a figure stepped from the shadows behind it. She dodged as it appeared in her peripheral vision, heading for the far side of the ramp instead of toward the car.

She was running full-out now, but still she couldn't avoid him. He leaped across the expanse that separated them and grabbed her upper arm, long fingernails digging into her flesh.

He jerked so hard that she stumbled against him. Unconsciously she put her hand on his chest in an attempt to regain her balance.

She was close enough now that she could smell him. Stale sweat and cigarette smoke. He put his other hand on her bare shoulder, dragging her to him so that her breasts brushed the stained T-shirt he wore.

As they did, she finally realized why they hadn't been tempted by the purse she'd thrown them. Apparently money had nothing to do with what they were after.

Chapter Two

Driven by panic and fury, Kelly ground the high heel of her sandal down on her assailant's toes. Luckily, he was shod in sneakers rather than the boots the others favored.

Hissing a profanity, he loosened his grip long enough to allow her to pull free. She started up the ramp again, intending to run to the next level, which she hoped would not be as deserted as this one.

Before she'd taken two steps, she heard the sound of a car. She looked up in time to see headlights appear at the top of the ramp. She ran toward them, waving her arms to attract the driver's attention. Surely he would take in the situation and stop to help her.

And what if he did? Always assuming it was a "he." It would still be four to one.

Four to two, she amended, feeling a ridiculous sense of triumph in the victory she'd achieved with her high heel.

Realistically she knew that the smart thing for whoever was in that car to do would be to drive past her. Just get the hell out of the parking deck. If she were lucky, he might stop somewhere and call the police. If the driver were another woman, that was almost certainly what would happen.

If it were a man, maybe he would slow enough to let her jump into the car as he went by. That would probably depend on whether or not she could put enough distance between herself and the boy who'd grabbed her to make that maneuver safe for the driver. Right now that was doubtful.

Even as she acknowledged the difficulty, the hand of the teen who had been hiding behind her car closed around the fabric of her skirt. She staggered forward, feeling the sheer material rip free from where it was attached to the bodice.

Desperation lent her strength. Somehow she managed to pull away from him. Once she had, she looked up again, trying to gauge how far she was from the approaching car.

She'd made almost no progress at all, she thought in despair. Then she realized the vehicle had stopped, its headlights shining down on the scene playing out below.

Her heart sank. Either this was a confederate arriving with the getaway car or the driver was rethinking his route.

Don't leave, she pled silently as she ran. *Please don't leave me alone with them.*

The sound of a car door slamming at the top of the ramp put an end to any hope of rescue. No one in his right mind, if he were an innocent bystander, would get *out* of that car. He might drive by at full speed. He might even back up to a higher level and park somewhere in the darkness, hoping the boys wouldn't come looking for him.

Those were options a normal person might take. Getting out of the car wasn't. Not in this situation.

As she ran toward the top, she could hear the sound of the driver's footsteps coming down the ramp. Slow, almost measured, they were suddenly the only noise on this level of the parking deck.

She turned from the blinding glare of the headlights to glance behind her. The four attackers had stopped their pursuit. Just as she was, they were listening to the approaching footsteps with a wary intensity.

Not a confederate then. This was something—*someone*—
totally unexpected.

She picked up speed as she ran toward the driver, hope
reviving her flagging strength. She didn't have breath
enough to scream for help. She had to trust that he'd as-
sessed the situation and figured out what was about to happen.

"What's going on here?"

The voice was deep and unbelievably calm. *Too* calm.
Maybe he *hadn't* understood. Maybe he'd just seen people
on the ramp and stopped to investigate.

As the man posed his question, he stepped toward the
center of the ramp. She could see him now, silhouetted
against the twin beams of the headlights. Tall and broad-
shouldered, he looked capable of holding his own in a fight.

"Help me," she gasped as she ran toward him.

He didn't look at her, focused instead on the teenagers
who were still watching from below. "Are you hurt?"

"No, but—"

"Get in the car."

That had clearly been an order, given in a tone that
brooked no argument. She didn't even think of making one.

She ran past him, her hand closing over the handle of
the passenger door of the black SUV he was driving. Before
she opened it, she looked back down the ramp.

The four had apparently recovered from their shock. Or
maybe they had finally realized there had been only one
person in this car and that he wasn't a cop or a security
guard.

They were advancing again. Slowly this time. From
somewhere a long iron bar had appeared.

Tire tool or crowbar, she guessed. The one who'd thrown
her purse aside held the instrument in his right hand, slapping it against the palm of his left. The whole thing looked

like something out of a bad production of *West Side Story,* but she didn't feel the slightest inclination to laugh.

"Get back into the car," she said to the man standing in front of the headlights. "Let's just get out of here."

There was no response. His stance, illuminated by the headlights, seemed completely relaxed.

"Please," she begged, beginning to be as afraid for him as she had been for herself. "We can lock the doors and drive by them. They can't hurt us if we're in the car."

No response. Maybe there was something wrong with him. Maybe he still hadn't realized what was going on. Maybe—

There was some sound from the group of teenagers. As if it had been a signal, they charged up the ramp in unison. The one holding the iron bar raised it high above his head, in full attack mode.

Sick with fear, she watched as they closed the distance to the solitary figure standing in front of the vehicle. She released the door handle and started back around the SUV. She had no idea what she could do, but she wasn't about to let him bear the brunt of that assault alone.

"I told you to get in the car," he said again, his voice as low and steady as it had been before.

And then, suddenly, they were there. She saw the raised crowbar begin its descent and knew its target. Too horrified to look away, she watched as it began to slice downward and then seemed to stop in midair.

The boy who wielded it staggered backward. With an agonized yell, he clutched his crotch with both hands. That's when she realized he was no longer the one holding the weapon.

It was being employed by the driver of the car instead. Although the headlights distorted the scene, so that it was almost like watching a flickering silent movie, she could still follow his movements. Shifting the weapon he'd taken from the first teen, he slammed the end of the bar into the ribs of a second, leaving him doubled over in agony.

In the time it had taken him to dispatch those two, the second pair had decided on a concerted effort. They attacked in unison before the man could get the crowbar into position to repel them. The momentum of their forward motion carried all three backward to slam onto the hood of the SUV. Kelly flinched at the hollow thud of their impact.

After that, given her position at the side of the car, she couldn't tell what was happening. All she knew was that two of the original four were still down and that the others were engaged in a fierce struggle with the driver of the SUV for possession of the weapon he'd taken away from their leader.

And that meant they were all occupied, she realized belatedly, their attention focused on him or on their injuries.

Her eyes flicked toward the elevator. Now was her chance to get out of here. While they were either distracted or in too much pain to care what she did.

The clang of the metal bar, striking and then bouncing off the concrete floor, brought her attention back to the bodies writhing on the hood of the car. She could hear the sound of blows as well as the noise their victim made as they impacted against flesh and bone.

She couldn't distinguish the recipient, but given the loss of the crowbar, she believed she knew who was getting the worst of the fight. No matter what happened to her, she couldn't run away without trying to aid the man who'd stopped to help her.

She bent down and slipped off one of her sandals, unable to think of anything else to use as a weapon. When she raised her head again, she saw that the three were no longer on the hood of the car. They were upright again, still exchanging blows.

Gathering what fragile courage she had left and feeling like a fool, she raised the flimsy shoe over her head and ran toward the struggling figures. Before she reached them, the two slighter bodies were propelled backward.

With room to maneuver, the driver, obvious both by his height and the breadth of his shoulders, began a series of lightning punches that drove his attackers back. His movements were so fast they were difficult to follow. She almost expected him to add a couple of martial arts kicks to the mix.

Apparently, he didn't need to. One of the two teens still on their feet broke away, running down the ramp with a clatter of boot heels. When the second realized he was about to have the driver's undivided attention, he also took off. His less noisy departure identified him as the one who had leaped across the ramp to grab her.

Having vanquished those two, the man advanced toward the first couple he'd dispatched. They weren't inclined to wait for him to reach them.

The one he'd kneed in the groin to take possession of the crowbar was still breathing in low, keening moans. His agony didn't prevent him from staggering to his feet and backing down the ramp, however, his eyes never leaving the driver. The second punk had his arms wrapped around his body, possibly the victim of broken ribs. If so, they didn't slow his retreat.

In a matter of seconds the parking level was empty except for her and the man who had just effected her rescue. In the sudden stillness she could hear the sound of his breathing. He swayed a little, but somehow managed to give the impression that he was both ready and able to take them on again if they returned.

Kelly realized she was simply standing, openmouthed at the speed and efficiency with which he'd detached the four attackers. She closed her mouth and started toward him.

Either he had incredible peripheral vision or very good instincts. He turned, dropping into a fighter's crouch. When he saw that she was the one who'd been moving behind him, he straightened.

"Are you all right?" she asked.

"What *is* that? Is that your *shoe?*"

Only then did she realize that she was still holding the sandal over her head, its heel pointing toward him.

"What the *hell* were you planning to do with your *shoe?*"

"Hit one of them," she answered truthfully.

Embarrassed, she lowered the feminine, near-nothing sandal he'd just belittled. Reaction was finally setting in. Her knees were shaking so hard she was in danger of falling flat on her face. She leaned tiredly against the hood of the SUV, tears threatening for the first time since the assault had begun.

She closed her eyes and took a deep breath. The first one she'd managed in quite a while.

It's okay. Everything's okay. Now isn't the time to fall apart.

"Are *you* all right?"

She opened her eyes to find him looming over her. Because they were standing between the beams of the headlights, she still couldn't see his face.

He was nothing but a shape, tall and broad. And a deep voice, filled with concern for her.

Which was ridiculous. *He'd* just taken a beating, and *she* was the one who was weak-kneed and weepy.

"If being scared spitless counts as okay." She hated that

her voice trembled, but there didn't seem to be much she could do about it.

"Spitless?" he repeated, the intonation amused as he emphasized the first syllable.

"Are they gone?" She ignored the mockery, feeling she had earned it. She looked back down the ramp, half expecting to see the attackers regrouping at its foot.

"They won't be back. They're the kind who like—"

"Easy pickings?" she supplied when he hesitated. If so, they'd come to the right place, she acknowledged bitterly.

"Obviously, they didn't know about the shoe."

The amusement was back, but she found she didn't resent it, even if it were at her expense. He was right. The sandal was a ridiculous weapon, but there *was* some justification for why she'd felt it might do some good.

"I ground my heel into his toe, and he let me go. I thought that maybe if I hit one of them with it—"

She sounded like an idiot. Actually, she felt like one.

"Thanks." The deep voice had been wiped clean of mockery. "There aren't many people who would have put themselves at risk to help."

"You did."

"Yeah, well, that's a failing of mine."

"Helping people?"

"I'm a sucker for a woman in distress."

For a fraction of a second she thought he'd said "a woman in a red dress." She must be more rattled than she'd believed.

"Why don't we get out of here," he suggested.

Since he'd used the plural pronoun, she wasn't sure if he meant individually or collectively. He didn't start around his vehicle to open the door for her to climb in, so she supposed he must mean in their own cars.

He took a long assessing look down the ramp and then

moved toward the driver's side of the SUV. In doing so, he passed directly in front of the beam of the left headlight.

"You were at the auction," she said, finally taking in the tuxedo.

"Sorry, but I didn't buy anything." He bent to retrieve the iron bar that had been lost in the scuffle, so she had to strain to hear the last. "A little too rich for my blood."

Since the guest list had been carefully screened to ensure that their checkbooks would be equal to the task before them, she wondered if that was his idea of a joke. She'd been introduced to most of the attendees during the cocktail hour, but she couldn't place him.

Could he be one of the wait staff? The big SUV he was driving made that unlikely, however, so who the hell was he?

After he retrieved the crowbar, he had continued past the driver's side door to open the back of the vehicle. He carelessly tossed the weapon inside. Then he straightened, looking at her over the line of the roof.

His face was still shadowed, but she couldn't help feeling there was something familiar about it. Maybe they *had* been introduced. After all, there had been a huge crowd of people.

"I'm Kelly Lockett."

It was a rather obvious attempt to evoke information. If he'd been there, he knew certainly who she was. She'd been paraded around that room like a sideshow for most of the evening.

"Of the Lockett Legacy. I know." The tone was sardonic.

"Do I know you?" she asked, reacting to it.

She had never been particularly self-conscious about the notoriety her family's wealth and prestige created. She had known nothing else her entire life, but something about that comment rankled.

"I was there on a friend's invitation. He said the food would be good."

"I trust you found that to be true," she said, a hint of ice creeping into her voice.

This man had rescued her, and she was genuinely grateful. Her initial inclination, which had been to view him as some kind of knight in shining armor, seemed to be fading.

Of course, she was well aware that most knights had been lacking in the courtly graces. Their forte had been the battlefield. She could hardly deny his skill there.

"You plan the menu?" He leaned forward, putting his arms on the top of the SUV.

"I was on the committee," she said stiffly.

"Could I make a suggestion?"

"About the *menu?*" There was something surreal about the conversation, considering what had just transpired.

"Fewer frills and more substance."

Despite her anger of a moment ago, she felt a tinge of sympathy. Dinner probably *had* seemed meager to a man his size. The appetizer had consisted of three large prawns, a dollop of crabmeat and a couple of avocado slices. The entrée, a nice piece of sole, had been surrounded by a selection of lightly sautéed vegetables. She had left food on her plate, but by no stretch of the imagination could the meal be called substantial.

"Steak and potatoes," she said, deliberately lightening her voice.

"It's hard to go wrong with a good steak. Especially at those prices."

"I'll ask the committee to take it under advisement," she promised, controlling her urge to smile.

"Almost makes me wish I could be at next year's shindig."

Something subtle about his intonation indicated he was aware she was patronizing him. It made her feel like a jerk.

"What happened to your shawl?"

"Stole," she corrected automatically, welcoming the change of subject.

Her eyes considered the concrete ramp that stretched in front of the SUV. Even with the headlights shining down it, she couldn't see a thin spill of red anywhere.

Her purse was also down there, she remembered. And more important, so was her wallet.

There was nothing in either that was irreplaceable, but it would be a hassle. Besides, they should still be there. She doubted those thugs had had the presence of mind after he'd finished with them to search for them on their way out.

"My evening bag's down there," she said. "Somewhere between the foot of the ramp and the elevator."

She turned her head, focusing again on the man in the darkness on the other side of the car.

"They snatched your purse?"

"I threw it to them. I thought maybe they'd take it and let me go, but…I don't think they were after money."

For some reason, she wasn't comfortable putting into words what she believed their motives were. Not to him.

"Maybe they wanted that."

He had inclined his head in her direction, but it took a couple of seconds before she figured out what he meant. She reached up to touch the replica of the diamond necklace Hepburn had worn in the movie. The central stone, had it been real, would have been between fifteen or twenty carats.

"It's paste."

"You think they knew that?"

It made sense. As much as anything about tonight.

"I'll get your purse," he said. He slammed the rear door of the SUV, the sound echoing under the overhang as the driver's side door had earlier.

Only when he started down the ramp did she realize she was about to be left up here alone. Although the headlights illuminated the ramp, the area behind his car was dark and shadowed. She shivered, remembering the hard fingers of the boy closing around her arm.

"I'll show you where he threw it."

She had already taken a step, attempting to catch up with him, before she realized she still held her sandal in her hand. It would take longer to put it on than to take the other off.

Balancing on one foot, she slipped the second shoe off as she watched him walk down the concrete incline. The fabric of the tux, illuminated by the car lights, emphasized the play of muscle in his back and shoulders. Regretfully pulling her eyes away, she laid her shoes on the hood of his car. Then, picking up her skirt as she'd done before, she hurried after him.

He slowed briefly, plucking her stole off the railing where it must have landed when she'd dropped it. Without stopping, he held it out to her. The wisp of fabric looked very delicate dangling from those long, dark fingers.

She grabbed the stole as he let it trail behind him and wrapped the material around her shoulders as he continued to stride ahead of her.

When he reached the end of the ramp, he turned toward the elevator area where there was more light. Apparently he spotted her bag and wallet at the same time she did.

She glanced nervously toward the outside exit to the deck, still expecting the reappearance of her assailants. When she looked back, the man who had rescued her had already picked up her belongings and was holding them out to her.

For the first time she could see his face. He was dark enough that there was already the shadow of a beard on his lean cheeks. A discoloration, which she suspected would become a very colorful bruise by morning, marred the line of his jaw.

She raised her eyes from that injury to meet his. A cut, still bleeding sluggishly, had been opened above his right brow. Under it, the eye was beginning to puff.

Despite that, a jolt like the one she'd felt as she'd met those same dark eyes while descending the runway stairs tonight seared a path like lightning through her chest.

Same eyes. Same force-field intensity. Same man.

Chapter Three

"I'm John Edmonds, by the way."

"Kelly Lockett."

He didn't make another jibe about her name, despite the fact that this was the second time she'd given it. She hadn't liked the crack he'd made before, and in all honesty, he couldn't blame her.

From everything he'd read, and that had been quite a bit since Griff had given him this assignment, she had never embraced the Lockett lifestyle. She might have rejected their example of conspicuous consumption, but it was clear, both by her comments from the dais about her brother and her reaction to his remark, that her rejection hadn't extended to her family.

"You told me," he said.

Watching her blush would have been highly diverting in other circumstances. The color started just above the top of the strapless gown and spread upward. It wasn't blotchy or unbecoming, just a flush of pink under the smooth porcelain of her skin.

It was increasingly obvious why they'd chosen the Hepburn gown for her. There was a resemblance both in the glossy, dark hair, arranged tonight in a classic French twist, and in those big brown eyes. And her features had the same kind of elegant purity.

The only difference was there was nothing in the least waif-like about Kelly Lockett. She was slim, but undeniably a woman. She filled out the bodice of the red dress in a way the actress never had.

"You should check that everything's there," he suggested, slightly lifting the purse and billfold he was holding out to her, one in each hand.

"He didn't want anything," she said, reaching out to retrieve them. "He thumbed through the money and then tossed the bag aside without taking it out."

As she described the boy's gesture, she repeated it, quickly counting the cash in the wallet's bill compartment.

"Not enough to be interesting?"

Her eyes came up at his question. "That's what I thought, but I'd forgotten that I cashed a check. There's a couple of hundred in here. Far more than I usually carry."

"Even if they were after the necklace, I would think they'd have taken it. That's not pocket change."

Or maybe it was for her. Still, it bothered him that those kids hadn't taken the money. It didn't make sense. Not even if they believed the necklace she was wearing was real. Not even if the motive had been something besides robbery, as she'd hinted.

"You said you didn't think robbing you was what they were after."

"The one who grabbed me…" she began and then faltered. "There was something… I don't know. It just felt… wrong."

"You thought he was going to rape you?" he asked bluntly.

Another hesitation. "I didn't know what he was going to do. I didn't like him touching me." Her shiver was strong enough to be visible. ''Maybe that was just my imagination.''

''They're gone now,'' he said, choosing to comfort rather than confront, although her instinctive assessment of the boy who had grabbed her was probably right on the money. ''Would you like me to follow you home?''

Her pupils dilated slightly. Shock? Or anticipation? *Yeah, right,* he mocked himself. *In your dreams.*

Then, almost immediately, wariness invaded her eyes. She was trying to decide if she wanted to tell him where she lived, unwilling to surrender even that much of her closely guarded privacy.

What she didn't know, of course, was that there was no secret about her address. Or about her any of her personal information. Not to someone with the sources he had.

He wasn't going to confess to those, however. There were too many things he *didn't* know about Kelly Lockett. And he had a feeling from what she'd said about her brother that there were a few things he knew that she might be completely ignorant of.

''I'm very trustworthy,'' he added, letting her hear his amusement.

''It isn't that…'' she began and then had the grace to pause, color moving along the line of her throat. ''You probably saved my life. At the very least you saved me from what would have been a highly unpleasant experience. How could I not trust you?''

''Easy. You don't know me. You don't know anything about me.''

Unconsciously as he talked, he put his fingers over the cut above his eye, which had begun to sting. He brought them away covered with blood. And it hurt like hell to move his jaw, he realized, experimenting.

"I know that you got that defending me." Her gaze touched on the injury beneath his brow.

"Reflex action."

"Thank you," she said softly. Her eyes had left their contemplation of the cut to refocus on his. "Not many people would have come to my aid. Not these days. You were very lucky they didn't have a gun."

"Hell, *they* were lucky I didn't have one."

Again her eyes widened. She was probably one of those people who believed nobody should carry a firearm, not even cops. Whatever ground he'd gained for knocking a few heads together on her behalf, he'd just destroyed.

"They were lucky *I* didn't have one."

It took a heartbeat for what she'd said to sink in. When it did, he laughed.

Her smile in response was nothing short of spectacular. He deliberately reminded himself of the advantages of being able to afford good orthodontic work and collagen injections. All the same, something hot and hungry stirred deep within his body.

"Actually, I'd be very grateful if you'd follow me home," she said. "And I'm pretty sure I've got a Band-Aid or two tucked away in a drawer somewhere."

Occasionally in this line of work things fell into your lap. No operative worth his salt turned down those opportunities. The going theory in intel was that it was better to be lucky than good. He couldn't argue with that. Certainly not in this case.

"Nurse Ratched, I presume," he said, bowing slightly.

"I believe Florence Nightingale is the analogy you're searching for," she corrected.

Her smile hadn't quite faded. And he knew he was going to be damned disappointed when it did.

"MAYBE I SHOULD give you directions in case we get separated."

"We won't," he promised, following her around the back of the vintage silver Jag. "Nice car."

"It was my brother's."

"The one you mentioned tonight?"

There was another of those telltale hesitations before she answered. "Chad."

"I'm sorry."

He was. More than she could imagine. Despite her attempts to keep her feelings private, it had been obvious at the auction that she'd been moved by that spontaneous tribute to her brother. And equally obvious that she was still grieving for him.

He imagined Bin Laden's family had loved him, too. That didn't necessarily mean they'd been unaware of his faults.

"Thank you," she said in response to his expression of sympathy.

She inserted the key into the driver's side door and opened it. The interior light came on, illuminating the darkness on this side of the Jag. It also revealed that the convertible was sitting at a peculiar slant.

He stepped back to check the rear tire, which, as he'd begun to suspect, was flat. As was the front.

"*That's* what he was doing back here," she said. "Letting the air out of the tires."

Her attackers had apparently left nothing to chance. Nothing except the one thing they couldn't control—that someone else might stumble onto the scene. And if he hadn't been watching her all night, he wouldn't have been aware of when she left. Considering her choice of exits, very few people at that party had been.

"Get a wrecker and have it towed," he suggested. "Unless you have *two* spares."

"No, but I do have a membership in a very good auto club."

She bent, putting her knee in the center of the leather driver's seat to reach across the low car. Red silk molded to a very nicely rounded derriere. *Definitely not waif-like,* he thought again.

She straightened, bringing a cell phone out of the car with her. "It wouldn't fit in my purse," she explained.

He pretended to examine the tires while she made the call.

"They say it's going to be a while."

He looked up to find her standing over him. Without rising, he pivoted on the balls of his feet to face her.

"How long?"

"Maybe an hour. They keep only two units on call this late, and they're both out."

"Let the brake off, lock it, and leave it to them. I'll drive you home."

He could tell she was torn. Maybe it was the thought of leaving the Jag to the mercies of some unknown wrecker service. Or maybe it was the thought of getting into a car with a stranger after what had happened tonight.

"I'm harmless, I promise," he added, willing to convince her.

Her lips tilted. It wasn't the smile that had dazzled him a few minutes ago. This one was more subdued, almost self-deprecating.

"Okay, but if I were you, I wouldn't call on the kids who did this to back up that claim."

She looked tired. And why shouldn't she be? he thought. It was nearly 3:00 a.m. She had been involved in the preparations for the auction since early this morning and for several days before. He knew that, because he'd been watching her since Griff had given him the assignment. A task he'd found extremely pleasant. Dangerously so.

And then she'd played Miss Social Butterfly all evening. He'd watched her do that, too, recognizing that it wasn't a role she was comfortable with. She'd gotten better as the night progressed, but it had been an effort.

"How about if I call you as a character witness instead?" he suggested.

"I know I'm being ridiculous—"

"Not after this," he interrupted, looking back at the deflated tires. "Look, if you want to wait—"

"I don't. I want to go home. I want to get out of these clothes…"

He would have bet that flush of color was again staining her throat. Despite the interior light in the Jag, he couldn't see her well enough to enjoy it this time.

"And into bed," she finished.

The last few words had spilled out in a rush. He suspected she'd intended to move away from the slightly suggestive remark she had made about taking off her clothes. It hadn't quite worked out that way.

"Release the brake and lock it," he advised again, ignoring the trap she'd laid for herself.

"Should we call the police? File a report or something?"

"Only if you want to spend the next couple of hours answering questions. Those kids are long gone, and on the scale of high priority crimes in D.C., this isn't even going to rank on the cops' list. They'll give the appearance of going after them, because of who you are, but they'll never make an arrest."

It wouldn't be to his advantage to have the cops show up, of course, but everything he'd just told her was the truth. Doing the paperwork on this would be a waste of time.

Putting his hand on the trunk of the car, he pushed himself to his feet with a small grunt of effort. The adrenaline that had flooded his system during the fight had faded so that he was beginning to feel the effects of the blows to the body he'd taken. He was fairly certain his ribs weren't broken, but he was going to be reminded of those baboons every breath he took for the next couple of days.

She had already leaned back into the car in order to follow his instructions about the emergency brake. Hearing that involuntary intake of breath, she straightened, looking back at him, instead.

"Sore?"

"Nothing a few aspirin and a long, hot shower won't fix."

"I can provide the aspirin. And the sooner you take them, the better. In the morning, you might want to get a doctor to take a look at—"

"I'm okay. I *will* accept the aspirin, however."

"As soon as we get to my place."

My place or yours? For a second or two her eyes held on his. Then she turned away, completing the motion she'd begun to release the parking brake.

Yes, sir, he thought, *sometimes things just fall into your lap. The problem then became knowing what to do with them when they did.*

"THROUGH HERE," Kelly directed, leading the way down a wide hallway.

There were photographs along each wall. He wanted to stop and check them out, because he recognized more than one famous face. She had already flicked on the light in a room a little farther along, however, and disappeared inside.

He followed, stopping in the doorway of a bathroom that was more than twice the size of his bedroom. There had been no expense spared in either the design or in the facilities. The round glass shower stall would have held a jury of his peers; the whirlpool, only a few less.

"Nice," he said.

He had refrained from comment as they'd made their way through the rest of the house. It had an understated elegance that, even to his untutored eyes, indicated it had been professionally, and expensively, decorated.

"The house was my brother's. I didn't see any sense in not using it while I'm in town."

She hadn't looked at him while she gave that information. She was busy searching through a cabinet that had been hidden behind a large panel of mirroring. He suspected the rest of the full-length wall of mirrors covered a variety of storage units. One by one she set the items she took from shelves down on the counter: gauze pads, alcohol, cotton balls, a tube of salve, a prescription medicine bottle, tape.

"It's a very small cut," he said as she continued to rummage.

She turned to look at him this time, her hand hesitating over the next selection.

"A Band-Aid's fine," he added.

"It needs to be cleaned. *They* weren't."

He was at a loss until he realized she meant the teens who'd attacked her. "The *kids* weren't clean?"

"Not the one who grabbed me. His shirt was dirty, and he smelled."

"Okay. *Alcohol* and a Band-Aid then."

"Followed by an antibiotic salve."

"Whatever floats your boat," he said agreeably.

He still couldn't quite believe he was here. As frightening as tonight's experience had been for her and as sore as he knew he was going to be in the morning, this had been an incredible stroke of luck. He didn't intend to blow it.

"I think the light's better over here."

Since you could have shot a movie in the place, he couldn't see what difference a few feet made, but obligingly he walked over to the area she'd indicated. She tilted the bottle of alcohol and poured some of it onto a cotton ball.

Its strongly antiseptic tang pervaded the pleasant scent of the room. Unthinkingly he tilted his head back, avoiding it.

"This will sting," she warned, moving toward him.

She was close enough now that, even above the bite of the alcohol, he could smell whatever perfume she was wearing. She reached up, bringing the soaked cotton ball near his forehead. He closed his lids to protect his eyes and braced for the burn.

It didn't come. After a couple of seconds, he cautiously opened his eyes to find that, although she was nearer than before, the hand holding the cotton ball still hovered in midair. Given the difference in their heights, she was at a distinct disadvantage.

"This would be easier if you sit," she suggested.

Obediently he settled one hip on the black marble counter behind him, keeping his other foot on the floor. He closed his eyes again, waiting. Still she hesitated, long enough that he finally opened them once more.

"What's wrong?"

She shook her head, moving forward until she was standing between his legs. The fragrance he'd noticed before, something dark, undoubtedly costly, and entirely suited to that strapless red gown, surrounded him.

''This is going to hurt,'' she warned again.

He hoped so. He hoped it hurt like hell. Enough to take his mind off what he was thinking. And if she got an inch or two closer, she was going to be in no doubt about the direction of his thoughts.

She put her free hand on his face, positioning her thumb under his chin, so she could turn it up to the light. He closed his eyes, determined to keep them that way as long as her cleavage was so temptingly near.

He wanted to bend his head and press his lips into the shadowed hollow between her breasts. To run his tongue along the top of that low-cut dress. He knew how her skin would taste.

The touch of the alcohol against the wound was cold and painful, exactly the distraction he needed. He flinched, pulling his chin away from her fingers.

''Sorry,'' she said, her warm breath feathering against his face. ''Just a little more, I promise.''

''It's okay,'' he muttered. ''It was just…cold.''

She dabbed at the wound again, more forcefully this time. When he didn't respond, she scrubbed away at the dried blood until the cut had been cleaned to her satisfaction.

She stepped back to survey her handiwork, allowing him an opportunity to open his eyes. Her face was right in front of him, although her gaze was still fastened on the injury.

''It's not too bad,'' she said, her eyes shifting to meet his.

He didn't know what they revealed about what he'd been thinking, but obviously something. Her lips parted, and she took a breath, deep enough to lift her breasts. He could see the pulse beating in her throat.

''You should probably have a stitch or two,'' she said, her voice thready.

"It's fine."

Again he raised his hand, intending to trace the cut in order to estimate the extent of the damage by feel. Her fingers quickly wrapped around his wrist, preventing him.

"You'll contaminate it," she said.

"Look, I don't think this is life-threatening…"

He hadn't intended to mock what she was doing. It was evident by the way her expression closed, however, that she had taken it that way.

"Just put some salve on it and tape it up," he said, modulating the impatience in his voice. "It'll be fine, I promise."

She nodded, but he could tell she was still hurt. *Way to go, idiot. You get the break of a lifetime, and you can't keep from being a smart-ass long enough to take advantage of it.*

She took a step back, tossing the bloodstained cotton ball into a small, gold-toned garbage can before she reached for the tube of antibiotic salve she'd set out. She removed one of the gauze pads from its cellophane wrappings and spread a generous layer of ointment across it.

Then she moved back into position between his legs. He had thought he was better prepared for her nearness this time, but when she leaned in, her hip rested against the inside thigh of the leg that was not in contact with the floor.

Heat flooded his groin. And this time there was no astringent bite to take his mind off the growing attraction.

She smoothed salve along his eyebrow, her concentration on the task nearly palpable. This time he didn't close his eyes.

Even from this proximity her skin was flawless. The smooth, perfect arch of her brows like wings. Her lashes incredibly long and dark.

After a few seconds she became aware that he was

watching her. Her eyes met his again as the hand holding the gauze pad stilled.

He waited for her to break the contact between them as she had before. When she didn't, he went with his instincts, leaning forward so that there were only a couple of inches between her lips and his.

Again he waited, giving her a chance to step back. To put her hand against his chest. To do anything that would signal this wasn't something she wanted, too.

Instead her chin tilted slightly upward. Her eyes closed, lashes falling like fans against her cheeks, as her lips parted.

There probably wasn't a man alive who wouldn't have taken advantage of the opportunity.

Certainly not this one.

Chapter Four

Her lips were exactly as he'd expected them to be. Soft and warm and responsive. And they opened willingly to the invasion of his tongue.

The resulting kiss was no tentative touch and retreat. It was long and deep and openmouthed, expressing a hunger they both seemed to feel. Some of the niggling guilt that he might be taking advantage of the situation began to fade as she moved into his arms.

After all, as far as he knew, she might be in the habit of picking up strange men and bringing them home. Women had long ago staked their claim to the same kind of sexual freedoms men enjoyed. In the back of his mind, however, lingered the memory of her blush and those faltering sentences about wanting to take off her clothes and get into bed.

Or maybe that had all been an act. If so, it was one she had perfected until it seemed genuine.

Some women felt the need to pretend innocence until they were ready to respond. It was a form of protection, and he respected it, but then when they did decide—

She shifted position, pressing her body along the length of his. He moved the hand that had been resting just below her waist lower, relishing the smooth slide of silk under his palm. Some part of him expected a gesture of reluctance, if only a token one, before she allowed that further intimacy. None came.

Not even when his fingers spread to cover the softly rounded curves he'd noted as she leaned into the Jag to retrieve her phone. His erection hardened at the memory.

Emboldened, he moved his other hand down until both were cupped over her bottom. He lifted slightly, pulling her up into the strength of his arousal.

A breath of surprise, or perhaps of pleasure, escaped her lips. Before he had time to decide which it had been, her fingers began to pluck at the knot of his black tie. She loosened it with a quick expertise, pulling it away from the collar of his shirt.

She dropped the strip of cloth somewhere behind her, her other hand already busy with the studs that secured his shirtfront. Her efforts to undress him were punctuated by the soft ping each stud made as it hit the stone countertop or the floor.

As soon as she'd removed enough of them, she slipped her hands inside his shirt, tugging at the cotton tee he wore beneath it. When it refused to come free from the waistband of his slacks, she broke the kiss, leaning back so she could look up into his face. Her mouth seemed swollen, excitingly well used, and her eyes were slightly glazed.

Passion? Or too much champagne? he wondered. Or, considering the day she'd had, maybe what he was seeing was sheer tiredness.

''Damn it,'' she said, putting her palms flat on his chest and pressing back against his hold.

Unsure what had happened to change the mood, he hesitated to release her. If they continued on the path they were on, the progression to being unclothed and together in a bed somewhere seemed almost certain.

And that was something he was vitally interested in right now. He wasn't sure they were yet to the point where someone wouldn't have second thoughts if they put some distance between them, even briefly.

Someone? he mocked. That assumed he was capable of second thoughts. Capable of *any* thought. And it was a huge assumption right now.

Rather than letting her go, he lifted his hip off the counter, keeping his hands under her buttocks. As he got to his feet, he allowed the front of her body to slide a couple of inches down his until she was again standing on the floor.

"Bedroom?" he suggested.

There was a flicker of something in her eyes. Before the emotion—whatever it was—could crystallize, he bent, putting his mouth over hers. This time he caressed her lips with a series of quick touches. A butterfly-light kiss on first one corner and then on the other before he turned his attention to the center of her mouth.

Meet and release. And then meet again. When he raised his head at last, her lips followed, clinging to his as she strained upward on tiptoe.

Reassured, he bent, placing one arm beneath her knees and the other behind her back. He lifted her easily, as if she weighed no more than a child.

When he turned to carry her out of that ornate bathroom, the wall of mirrors revealed multiple reflections of the red silk dress, its color vivid against the stark black and white of his tuxedo.

WHEN HE PICKED HER UP to carry her into the bedroom, Kelly had laid her head against his shoulder. She'd closed her eyes, consciously deciding not to examine what was happening between them too closely.

She certainly recognized that was a form of denial, but it was one she didn't try to resist. Given everything that had happened during the past two months, this man's arms seemed a haven of security in a world that had contained far too little of either. Tonight she had watched him take on four thugs on her behalf, and his body bore the marks of that encounter.

Despite the fact that he had given her every chance to back away from this, she hadn't wanted to. She would have if he'd tried to rush or coerce her. Because he hadn't, she had almost become the aggressor, a role she had never assumed before.

She didn't want him to leave. She could not bear to be alone again. She didn't want to lie in that big, lonely bed another night thinking about the crushing responsibilities that had resulted from Chad's death.

And she also didn't want to think about what had nearly happened tonight. Actually, she didn't want to think about anything. All she wanted to do was to feel.

Someone's arms around her. Someone strong enough to depend on. Someone she could trust.

She had trusted John Edmonds immediately. Instinctively. And so far he hadn't betrayed her faith in him. At every juncture, he had left the important decisions up to her. Just as he had this one.

Allowing a man she didn't know to spend the night was not a choice she would normally have made, but as John carried her toward the bedroom, she knew it was right. He had been willing to risk his life to protect hers. And he had done it at no small cost to himself. There was something infinitely appealing about that. Something noble and heroic.

Heroism. It was a concept most of the people she'd met in Washington would probably believe to be hopelessly out of date. Maybe it was, but she had responded to his offer of protection as women had responded throughout the centuries. If that made her weak, then so be it.

Tomorrow she would again shoulder the burden that had been thrust upon her by her brother's death because she had no choice. For tonight—for these few brief hours—she wanted only to be held. To be rendered mindless. To be loved.

JOHN HAD BEEN SURPRISED at how little she was wearing under the red silk gown. Of course, the way the dress was cut as well as its fit precluded the possibility of many undergarments.

There was only a thong, nude-colored and very sheer. When he unzipped the dress, letting it slide down over her hips, for an instant he thought she literally had on nothing at all.

She had stepped out of the spill of fabric at her feet wearing only that nearly invisible wisp of cloth and the fragile sandals she'd tried to use against the attackers. The memory of her coming to his defense armed only with that ineffective weapon gave renewed life to the guilt he'd managed to bury.

Kelly Lockett might have more money than the budgets of most third-world countries, but she also had guts. And she hadn't fallen apart when it was over, despite the condition of the Jag.

He had known a lot of men who would have ranted about the inconvenience of those flat tires. Instead, she had accepted that the car was damaged and had taken steps to deal with it. Just as she'd adjusted to everything that had been thrown at her tonight.

He was too accustomed to making on-the-spot assessments not to have already formed an opinion of this woman. And so far his feelings had all been positive. Since he had long ago learned to listen to his intuition about people, he was beginning to believe that whatever kind of scumbag her brother might have been, Kelly had known nothing about it.

"What's wrong?"

Her question brought him out of his reverie. The few seconds he'd spent not holding her in his arms had, however, reminded him of why he was here. This had definitely not been part of the assignment he'd been given. All he had been told to do was surveillance.

Of course, Griff couldn't have imagined that this opportunity would arise. And that *was* the operative word, he reminded himself. *Opportunity*.

That inconvenient sense of guilt brushed through his mind once more. If Ethan Snow were correct in what he suspected, however, the end would more than justify the means. Even Griff would have to agree with that assessment.

"Wrong?" he echoed softly before he stepped forward to gather her into his arms. "Not a single thing."

HE LOWERED HIS HEAD, pressing his lips against the dew of perspiration at her temple. The long, dark hair had long ago released from the upswept style the fashion show required. Silken strands tangled around their entwined bodies like a net, binding him to her as they had made love.

Once with a heated frenzy driven by *her* demands, *her* need. And then this second time, a slow, lingering seduction during which he had explored every scented millimeter of her body. Satin-skinned, it was also incredibly well toned. And so damned responsive. She had refused him nothing, but there had been no doubt in his mind that *he* was making love to *her*.

Her eyes were closed as he touched her. At least there

were no tears gathered beneath her lashes as there had been the first time. Looking down on them, for one terrifying heartbeat, he had believed that he had inadvertently hurt her.

Of course, the fury with which he'd taken her then had been at her instigation. She had urged him on with her words and her body, leaving him in no doubt of what she wanted. And her eventual climax had been as wild and unrestrained as his own.

When it was over, however, when he had finally found the strength to open his eyes again, she'd been crying. It was not until he had brushed his thumbs over the moisture that she'd opened her eyes and looked up at him.

She shook her head in answer to his unspoken concern, but she hadn't protested when he'd rolled onto his back, carrying her with him. He had held her against his side a long time, neither of them speaking. Her head had rested on his shoulder, her hand relaxed on his chest.

He had thought she was asleep until he'd moved, trying to find a more comfortable position for his battered body. She had risen on one elbow and leaned over him. She had stared down into his face for a long time before she bent her head, her mouth again seeking his.

That kiss was what had led to this unhurried exploration of her body. Using his hands, his mouth, and his tongue, he had marked it with his touch—from the sweet, silken curve of her breasts to all the shadowed places nature had so carefully guarded.

"Yes," she breathed.

In response, he lowered his head again, his tongue caressing the last intimacy. Her fingers clenched and then loosened their hold on his hair as he touched her, his movements unhurried.

All the time in the world.

Her breathing gradually changed, becoming faster and more ragged. Small, nearly soundless inhalations gave way to deeper ones, until finally the air rushed in and out of her open mouth as if she were running a race.

As soon as he felt the first delicate shudder rack her frame, he moved into position over her body. His first downward thrust corresponded to her long, involuntary intake of breath, almost a moan.

He needed no other encouragement. As her hips lifted to meet his, his own release began. They clung to one another as wave after wave of sensation washed through their straining bodies.

Mindless now, he never even thought about who she was or why he was here. This wasn't about the Phoenix or an assignment or surveillance.

This was only about a woman whose hands clung to him as she trembled beneath him. A woman who whispered his name, even in the throes of her own fulfillment. A woman who matched him movement for movement until they had climaxed together.

Finally the sexual storm passed, leaving him again too drained to move. Only then did he realize that the dynamics of what he was supposed to do had been inevitably changed by what had just happened between them. Like it or not, Kelly Lockett was no longer just the sister of the man he had been sent to investigate.

Innocent bystander or in it up to her neck, she was also a woman to whom he had just made love. And that would impact every other decision he'd make during the course of this assignment.

Chapter Five

Kelly came awake abruptly, with an undefined, but very real sense that something was wrong. She realized from the intensity of the sun against the drawn drapes that the morning was well advanced.

She closed her eyes against the glare, aware of a dull ache at the back of her head. Too little sleep, she thought, which wasn't unusual these days.

And then she opened them again, the memories of last night flooding her newly awakened consciousness like a bad dream. The tensions of the auction. The attack in the parking deck. The rescue. *The rescuer.*

She sat up in bed, changing the ache into pain. The other side of the mattress was empty, but the sheets had been disturbed. And the pillow still bore the impression of a head.

Not a dream, she acknowledged. *A nightmare.*

She surveyed the room, looking for evidence that might indicate whether or not he was still in the house. The dress she had modeled was a crimson puddle against the thick, white bedroom carpet. Her sandals lay on their side by the bed. And her underclothes...

She had no idea where they were. She did have an unforgivably clear recollection of their removal.

She took a breath, fighting her growing sense of panic. The entire episode seemed unreal, from the attack in the parking deck to what had happened in this room last night.

What the hell had she been thinking? What the hell had she been *doing?* That was the far more important question. And the other one, equally important right now: Where was he?

Her gaze circled the room again, finally locating what she'd been looking for. Neatly arranged on a chair was a tuxedo. The pants had been hung over one arm, the satin stripe along the leg dully reflecting the sunlight. The jacket was draped across the back, emphasizing the width of its shoulders. Since they were still here, that meant—

She took another breath, fighting for calm, and realized she was trembling. It had been a very long time since she'd made love. Last night she had chosen to do so with a stranger. And she couldn't begin to explain why.

The emotional release at having gotten through the auction, maybe. A sense, right or wrong, that she had finally paid her dues to Chad's memory and that it was time to get on with her own life? If so, this seemed a hell of a way to begin.

Or maybe what had happened last night had been rooted in her genuine gratitude to the man who had risked his life to save hers. Despite the regret she felt this morning, she had to admit there had been an incredible feeling of security at being held in his arms. One she hadn't known for months.

She had slept like a baby. *After* they'd made love.

Made love. It was a term people threw around as if it meant something. In this case it didn't.

She could call it whatever she wanted, of course. Dress it up in the most palatable terms, but what had happened last night had had nothing to do with love. And they had both known it.

Tiredly she used her fingers to comb her hair away from her face. It was tangled, beginning to return to its stubborn natural curl. Using both hands, she began to gather it at the back of her neck, intending to loop it into a knot to get it out of her way. At some point in those familiar, unthinking movements, she became aware of her nudity.

Her hands released the tumbled strands, allowing them to fall over her shoulders again. She listened to the almost eerie silence of the huge house. Despite the fact that John Edmonds's clothes were still here, it felt as if she was alone.

She slipped out of bed, resisting the urge to grab the coverlet off the foot to wrap around her naked body. Instead, she hurried across the room to the closet.

She opened the door and walked into what was actually a fair-size room, with built-in drawers and storage compartments and two long revolving clothes racks. The garments she had brought with her from Connecticut occupied a few inches of space at the end of one of them.

Frantically pushing hangers aside, she grabbed the first thing she came across that would provide instant coverage. It was the knee-length cotton robe she sometimes changed into after work. She lapped the sides tightly over her breasts and then belted it around her waist.

In addition to her headache, she was cognizant of a slight soreness in her lower body. Since her remembrance of what had happened last night was now crystal clear, including her own behavior, this morning's discomfort was surprising only in that it wasn't more unpleasant. And she could hardly blame him for that tenderness.

Actually, there was little blame for any of this that she could lay at his door. She had invited him in. She hadn't refused the first overture he'd made. Or any of the others, she admitted, feeling heat climb into her cheeks. Not one single time had she said no.

The expectations she had created by her acquiescence to his every desire would have to be dealt with this morning. The sooner the better.

She recrossed the bedroom, headed toward the hall. When she reached the doorway, she paused, looking up and down it.

Again she listened. This time she identified the sound she must have been hearing subliminally now for several seconds. And when she thought about it, that he would be there wasn't surprising.

Without giving herself time to think better of the confrontation, she walked along the hall in the direction of the noise. As she neared its source, her heart rate accelerated until she could feel the pulse of blood beating in her temples.

There was nothing to be nervous about, she told herself. She'd done nothing to be ashamed of. She was single and over twenty-one. And it was the twenty-first century. She didn't owe anyone an explanation for whomever she let into her bed.

No one except herself. She had always been her own most damning critic, and she hadn't yet figured out an explanation for this situation she was willing to accept.

He had left the door to the bathroom open, so the sound of the jets grew louder as she neared it. She swallowed again before she stepped through the doorway and found him exactly where she'd expected him to be—in the whirlpool, his dark head resting on one of the cushions along the rim.

Given the fact that she was barefoot and the jets were going full blast, he couldn't possibly be aware she was here. That meant she would have a few seconds to compose what she needed to say.

"Good morning." The same deep voice that had ordered her into his car last night put a quick end to that fantasy.

From this angle, his position didn't appear to have changed. He must have made some slight movement, however. It was repeated a dozen times in the gold-glazed mirrors that tiled the ceiling, drawing her eyes upward.

They met his in the glass. Even in that imperfect reflection, she could see that the area under the cut on his brow was dark, the eyelid swollen nearly shut.

She'd also been right about the colorful nature of the bruise on his jawline. There were additional contusions on the broad chest as well, clearly visible where the swirl of dark hair and bubbling water didn't hide them.

"I hope you don't mind," he said. "I didn't want to wake you to ask permission."

The propulsion of air through the water was forceful enough that nothing below the line of his nipples was visible in the mirrors. Still, she lowered her gaze from the ceiling, focusing it resolutely on the back of his head.

She had come here to speed him on his way. Despite the sense of self-recrimination she'd felt when she opened her eyes to the impression of his head on the pillow beside her, she was remembering the feel of his hair beneath her fingers. And the sweet, hot touch of his mouth against her body.

Blocking that memory, she licked dry lips. "How are you?"

A brilliant bit of conversation. Of course, she wasn't up on what one said to a strange man with whom one had just spent the better part of the night and to whom one had allowed unlicensed intimacy. Probably because she had never before found herself in this position.

"Just like I told you last night. Nothing aspirin and a long, hot soak won't remedy."

She remembered offering him aspirin—along with everything else—but she believed the original sentiment had had to do with showers rather than baths. What the hell did that matter? After the fight he'd mounted against her attackers, he had a right to whatever form of water therapy he chose. She was very grateful that the soreness she felt this morning had been the result of—

Consensual sex. The familiar phrase jarred, but at least it was accurate. Thanks to him.

"You hungry?" he asked.

The non sequitur caught her off guard. "I beg your pardon?"

"I make a mean omelette. If you've got eggs."

She wasn't sure what the big refrigerator held. She hadn't done a lot of eating since she'd been here. No more than she had managed a lot of sleep.

Last night, however, she had done exactly that. She had slept. Peacefully and without nightmares.

And she was hungry, she realized, almost with a sense of wonder. The "I've worked hard and my body needs fuel" kind of hunger she couldn't remember feeling in the weeks she'd lived in this monstrosity of a house.

If there weren't eggs in the fridge, they could order some in. There was a grocery store nearby that delivered. Chad had the number written on the memo board in the kitchen.

"I don't know," she said, stalling while she considered her options.

She had come into the room determined to get him out of the house as fast as she could. She'd been embarrassed about last night. Angry with herself for letting the emotional upheaval of the past two months lead her into such an uncharacteristic situation. Now she was actually considering allowing him to stay for breakfast. What kind of hold did this man have on her?

Her gaze flicked up to the mirrors on the ceiling again. He was watching her, his face impassive.

Maybe if it hadn't been for that black eye. Or the bruises on his chest and shoulder. Maybe…

"There's a place that delivers," she heard herself say. It was almost as if the words had no relation to her. As if they were coming out of someone else's mouth. "I think I've got the number somewhere."

He nodded, still holding her eyes. "I'll meet you in the kitchen."

HE'D HAD A PRETTY GOOD IDEA what she'd been thinking when she walked into the bathroom. Since she hadn't carried out her intention immediately, however, he wasn't going to give her an excuse to get rid of him now.

When he entered the kitchen less than ten minutes later, he was dressed in the pants of the tuxedo and his T-shirt. He would have been here a lot quicker if he hadn't made the mistake of trying to locate enough of those damned studs to fasten the evening shirt. Not that he'd succeeded.

She was buttering bread, still wearing the robe that left long shapely calves exposed. She looked up at his entrance and then went back to the task at hand. On the counter next to the stove, several items had been laid out, including a carton of eggs, fresh mushrooms, cheese and a hand-held grater.

"That's it, I'm afraid. Unless you want me to call the grocer."

"This is good for me," he said, breathing in the aroma of freshly brewed coffee.

He walked over to a space-age-looking carafe surrounded by an equally futuristic coffeemaker. As he poured coffee into the mug she had set out beside the contraption, he studiously avoided looking at the numbers on the memo board she'd mentioned, which was hanging nearby.

He took his first sip of coffee, turning his back on the carafe. Kelly had finished preparing the toast and was placing each buttered slice neatly on a baking sheet that looked as if it had never been used.

While she put that into the oven, he selected a knife from the butcher-block holder beside him. He moved back to the counter beside the stove and began chopping the mushrooms. When he had grated the cheese, he whisked the eggs and added the other ingredients.

Then he dropped a pat of butter into the omelette pan he'd taken from the rack above the island cook top. Just as he poured the egg mixture into the browning oil, aware of his audience throughout the process, the doorbell rang.

He looked up, raising a questioning brow. "Expecting company?"

She shook her head without answering. She took time to pull the lapels of her robe more closely together before she disappeared through the kitchen doorway.

Chained to the stove by the omelette, John listened as voices drifted back from the front of the house. One of them was clearly masculine.

Delivery? he wondered, tilting the pan as he lifted the edge of the browning eggs. That would be unusual on a Sunday morning. Or maybe it wasn't, if money was no object.

He had a few seconds' warning that whoever had rung the bell was being brought back to the kitchen when the voices suddenly grew louder. At least the male one did.

It sounded a little too cheery. Falsely so.

Kelly's face as she entered revealed that she wasn't pleased about the invasion. He suspected her unhappiness wasn't because she saw it as an intrusion on their time together, but because she was embarrassed to have her visitor find a man in her kitchen. It would be obvious by their dress that he'd spent the night here.

"She tried to keep me out, but I was irresistibly drawn by the smell of coffee."

The intruder was a man of about John's age, in his late thirties or perhaps his early forties. He was wearing a pale-blue golf shirt tucked into gray slacks. A black alligator belt emphasized the trimness of his waist as well as the muscled chest above it.

His hair, dark and long enough to touch his collar in the back, was brushed with gray at the temples. His skin had the kind of deep, even tan that didn't come from a bottle.

John put the pan down and half turned from the stove to take the hand the visitor had offered. He found its palm hard and callused, the handshake firm. Sailing or tennis, he guessed. Maybe polo. Something that demanded a lot of time in the sun as well as good physical condition.

"Mark Daniels," the visitor said. "Enough of that for three?"

A *very* old friend, John decided, his gaze moving from that friendly, open smile to the closed face of his hostess before he returned the introduction.

"John Edmonds."

"I don't think I've seen you around," Daniels said, releasing his hand to amble over to the coffeemaker. "From out of town?"

The question, thrown over his shoulder, was phrased in a slight Southern accent. Its tone said idle curiosity. The clear blue eyes said something quite different.

"Originally. I've been in the area for about ten years."

There was a brief silence while Daniels poured his coffee. John took the opportunity to look at Kelly again, but she shook her head. One quick decisive movement.

"I thought maybe you'd come down from Connecticut to visit Kelly. I'm sure she's been missing her friends while she's been here taking care of Chad's business. You knew Chad, of course?"

"No, he didn't. We only met last night," Kelly interrupted, her voice flat.

"At the auction? Funny, I don't remember your name from the guest list."

"A friend gave me his invitation," John said easily. "He couldn't make it."

"I see. I didn't realize the bidding was quite that fierce," Daniels said, raising his cup to his lips. He looked at John over the rim. "You the winner or the loser?"

He meant the black eye. It might have been polite to ignore it, but not if you were seeking information.

"I had some trouble on the way to my car," Kelly said. "John...helped."

"What kind of trouble?" The jovial tone had disappeared.

"Some kids. Teenagers. They tried to snatch my purse."

John wasn't surprised she downplayed what had happened. She didn't strike him as someone who liked to talk about her problems. Or maybe she just resented Daniels's overt curiosity.

"Where?"

"In the parking deck," John said. "I happened to be driving out at the time and saw them."

"And came to the rescue," Daniels said admiringly, the accent thicker than it had been before. "It seems then we are in your debt, Mr....Edmonds, was it?"

Only a minute ago he'd been sure John's name wasn't

on the guest list. It seemed unlikely he'd forgotten it in the meantime.

"That's right."

"Well, lucky for all of us that you were there."

John ignored the royal plural, which sounded proprietary. For some reason that set his teeth on edge.

Using the eggs as a distraction, he turned back to the cooktop. He slipped a plate under the pan, sliding the omelette onto it. After he'd set it down on the stove, he opened the oven door, using the mitt Kelly had laid out to remove the toast. He turned to find Daniels watching him. The smile was no longer in evidence.

"I take it you're joining us." John made sure there was no hint of welcome in his voice.

"Thanks, but I really don't have time. Just needed my caffeine fix. Mind if I take the cup?" The last was directed at Kelly and punctuated by a small lift of the mug he was holding.

"Be my guest," she said.

"I'll see myself out. Don't let your food get cold, you two. Enjoy."

Daniels walked toward the door, but neither of them moved to do what he'd suggested. When he reached the doorway, he spoke directly to Kelly.

"We need to talk. Let me know when it's convenient."

The cool blue eyes touched briefly on John's face before Daniels left the kitchen. He hadn't bothered to say goodbye. Maybe because he hadn't liked the answers he'd gotten to his questions.

They waited together until they heard the front door close. Even after it had, there was a waiting stillness in the kitchen. Whatever ease sharing breakfast might have provided to the natural tension between them had effectively been destroyed, and they both knew it.

"Did I say something wrong?"

Her eyes considered his face before she shook her head. "Mark fancies himself Chad's successor."

"With the Legacy?"

"With me. Chad was my big brother. Mark was his best friend. He thinks that puts him under some kind of obligation to assume the role."

"He objects to me being here because he thinks Chad would have?"

Maybe he'd been wrong about what had happened last night being her usual modus operandi. Apparently she wasn't in the habit of bringing strangers home. At least not since she'd been in Washington.

"What he doesn't understand is that Chad and I argued because he refused to give up that role long after it was appropriate. If I didn't accept Chad's right to tell me what to do, I don't intend to accept the right of someone who has far less reason to interfere."

"I take it he's tried?"

Her mouth tightened, but again she didn't answer. He'd been right. She really *didn't* like talking about her problems.

"Are you going to eat that?" she asked instead, inclining her head toward the plate that held the eggs.

"It seems a shame to let it go to waste."

"I have a meeting," she said.

"With Daniels?"

"With the hotel. A rehash of what went wrong and what went right last night. I volunteered to do it and let the rest of the committee sleep in."

"What time?"

She glanced at the clock on the wall, and his gaze followed. It was almost eleven.

"At one."

"Time enough to eat," he said.

"You eat while I get dressed."

"I can drop you off."

Her lips parted, almost certainly to issue a denial, and then she closed them. She had apparently forgotten she didn't have a car.

"I'll call the auto club and check on the condition of the Jag while you're getting ready," he offered. "They can bring it to wherever you'll be."

She was thinking about it. Given the time frame, the only other option would be for her to take a cab. And it was a long trip.

"Thank you," she said finally. "The meeting is at the same hotel. Tell them to leave it with the parking valet in my name."

The acceptance of his offer was grudging. She began to turn away as soon as she'd made it.

"One bite."

She looked back at him and then down at the omelette.

"I can make you a sandwich," he offered. "Portable breakfast. Eat it while you run your bath."

"Shower," she corrected. "I take showers."

"Pity," he said softly.

She looked up, those big brown eyes widening slightly.

"It wasn't my fault he showed up this morning," he said.

"I know."

"And it's really not too late to salvage breakfast."

She thought about that one, too, but not as long. "Actually, it is, but...thanks for trying."

"Rain check?"

Another pause. Her eyes held on his.

"Maybe...dinner?" he suggested.

It had been obvious she was having second thoughts

about what had happened last night. It was time to back up and punt. And he wasn't averse to courting the lady.

"I'd like that," she said, surprising him, before she turned and disappeared through the kitchen doorway.

Chapter Six

He ate most of the omelette standing in front of the sunlit windows before he called about the car, arranging for it to be delivered to the hotel. Then he poured another cup of coffee and thought about what, if anything, he'd accomplished.

Surveillance was all he'd been charged to do, and he had far exceeded that directive. However no one, not even Griff, could argue that he wasn't in a better position this morning to check out the possibility that charitable donations to the Lockett Legacy were being used to fund terrorist activities than he had been yesterday.

"What did they say?"

He turned from his unseeing contemplation of the scene outside to find Kelly standing in the kitchen doorway. Head tilted to one side, she was struggling to fasten the second of a pair of gold earrings. Other than that, she appeared ready to walk out the door.

Her dress was one of those deceptively simple knit things that had probably cost hundreds of dollars. It was the dark red of a good burgundy. With it she wore black low-heeled pumps and no jewelry other than the earrings. She held a black leather purse, much larger than the tiny envelope she'd carried last night, under her arm while she worked.

"Need some help?"

"I can get it. It's being difficult because I'm in a hurry. The automobile club?" she prodded.

"They'll have the car at the hotel by one-thirty."

She nodded, having finally managed to secure the plain gold hoop. "Thank you. Thank you for everything. Last night—"

"Anybody would have stopped," he interrupted, uncomfortable with her gratitude. After all, he had had a vested interest in coming to her rescue.

"No, they wouldn't. I know that and so do you. Even if they had, not everyone would have been able to handle them. Do you have some…law enforcement experience or something?"

"Military," he said. That was true, even if it wasn't the entire story.

She nodded. "If I didn't fully express my appreciation last night—" She stopped again, that sweep of color betraying her realization of the interpretation that could be made of those words. "That *wasn't* what last night was about. What happened here, I mean."

"What *was* it about?"

It was a question no gentleman should ask. He should have accepted her explanation and moved on. That was probably what she'd expected when she made it. Once it had been asked, however, she didn't avoid the question.

"A lot of things, I think. Being in Washington alone for so long. Having the auction over after weeks of worrying about how it would go. Maybe even the fact that it was such a success. I *was* grateful for what you did, but that wasn't why it happened. Everything just seemed…"

He waited for her to go on. When she didn't, he set down his mug and walked across the kitchen. She watched his approach, the wariness back in her eyes.

He put his hands on her shoulders, intending to pull her to him. Today she made no effort to meet him halfway. She simply looked up at him instead.

After a few seconds he lowered his head, barely touching her lips with his. When he straightened, still holding her shoulders, her eyes were closed, the lashes once more lying motionless against her clear skin. Unwillingly he remembered last night's tears.

"Dinner," he said.

Her eyes opened to search his face. "Not tonight," she said. "I can't tonight."

He knew it was a lie, but he didn't press the point.

"Whenever you're ready." He held his breath until she nodded. "I'll write my number on the memo board."

The only business cards he had on him identified him with the Phoenix. The name of the investigation agency would probably mean nothing to her, but if she were curious enough to do some research, she might find out more than he was prepared to reveal right now.

She nodded and moved her shoulders, a subtle attempt at withdrawal. He removed his hands, freeing her immediately.

"I have to get my briefcase," she said. "It's in the office."

"I'll collect the rest of my things and meet you out front."

He thought about mentioning the missing studs and then decided that would be treading on dangerous territory. In the cold light of day, she seemed to want to disavow her role in what had happened between them last night. Or at least to relegate it to the realm of something that had occurred because of emotional overload. Maybe she was right, but the idea didn't make him feel any better.

If she didn't call him, he would eventually initiate contact. He would give it a day or two before he did. It would be better for any number of reasons if she phoned him. And it would certainly be better for his peace of mind.

THE WOODEN BLINDS were still closed in the office, providing an artificial twilight to the big room. Rather than turning on the lights, she walked across and pulled the cord, sending slanting lines of sunlight across the surface of the desk.

It was here that she felt closest to Chad. Maybe because this was the heart and soul of the charitable empire he had built and ruled until his death. A kingdom built on the Biblical philosophy their grandfather had espoused: From those to whom much has been given, much is expected.

She had set her briefcase down on the floor when she'd come in yesterday. She picked it up now and put it on the top of the desk. Opening it, she checked to make sure she had everything she needed for today's meeting.

The printout of the contract and a dozen other things she had had to keep up with during the past two months were neatly arranged in tabbed folders. She had been so new to all this that it had taken a huge commitment of organization on her part to keep all those balls in the air at the same time. Thankfully, it seemed she had dropped none of them.

She closed the case and then picked it up in preparation for leaving. Her gaze skimmed over the surface of the desk to make sure there wasn't anything there she had forgotten.

She had already turned away when the aberration registered. Her eyes came back, again considering the few items on the desktop, the crucial one a box of multicolored disks.

Chad had kept a lot of information on this computer. It was here she had come to try to understand the intricacies of the foundation her brother had run so successfully. Although she had found what appeared to be a complete financial statement for the Legacy, it had been Chad's simplified version she'd relied on to get a handle on what was taken in and where it went.

As she'd gone through his material, she had downloaded information about each charity onto a different-colored disk to help her keep track of them. It had quickly become apparent that one of the funds had gotten far more of Chad's attention than the rest, especially during the final two months of his life.

The last time she'd worked in here, there had been several of each of the other colored disks left in the box, but only two of the reds, which she'd been using to download information about The Covenant. Now there was one.

She tried to think if she had used the computer at all since she'd noticed there were only two red disks remaining, but she knew in her heart that she hadn't. The past several days had been taken up with endless preparations for the auction. Everything else had been put on hold, including her review of the Legacy finances.

Just in case she was wrong, she pressed the eject button on the tower. Nothing happened. The missing disk wasn't in the computer.

And if *she* hadn't taken it out of the box, that meant someone else had. The only reason someone would have for doing that—

The realization was stunning. As a precaution, she opened each of the drawers of the unlocked desk in turn. Nothing appeared to be disturbed, but the missing disk was in none of them.

Aware of time passing as she searched, she closed the last drawer with a growing sickness in the pit of her stomach. Chad had always said she was too trusting. Obviously he'd been right.

And now, to keep from letting John Edmonds—or whatever the hell his name was—know that she had discovered what he'd done, she was going to have to get into that big SUV with him and let him take her to the hotel. She took a deep breath, attempting to control her anger.

She picked up her briefcase again and headed to the front door. Last night had been an even bigger mistake than she had imagined, but at least it had given her a place to start.

This was the first slipup they'd made. And she was determined to use it to her advantage.

"IT APPEARS THAT once the expenses have all been paid, last night's event will garner more than eight million dollars for the foundation," Hugh Donaldson said. "That means, ladies and gentlemen, that this auction was the largest single moneymaker since the beginning of the Legacy."

The applause around the huge conference table varied in degrees of enthusiasm. As Kelly's gaze scanned the faces of the board members who had gathered on this Sunday afternoon for a post-mortem of the fundraiser, she found no surprises in who had greeted the results with delight and in those whose appreciation was mitigated by their dissatisfaction with the way the charity was being administered. The schism had surfaced at the first meeting she'd sat in on after Chad's death.

At that time she had been a reluctant participant, still grief stricken and nearly oblivious to the infighting going on around her. After dealing with it for more than two months, she felt that she knew exactly who stood where.

"Thank you, Hugh," Catherine Suttle said.

A lifelong resident of the Beltway, Catherine was reputed to know everybody who was anybody in the capital. That apparently gave her the right to call the senior partner of Donaldson Accounting by his first name. It was something Kelly wouldn't have done, although Hugh and Chad had been very good friends.

Of course, she had discovered that was the case with most of those who sat on this board. Their first loyalty hadn't been to the foundation, but to the man who started it. Unfortunately, their goodwill hadn't necessarily transferred to his heir.

One exception had been Catherine. As chairman of this year's auction, she had proven to be a font of helpful information. Although a volunteer, like the others on the board, she had been with the foundation in one role or another since the beginning. More than once Kelly had gone to her with questions she hadn't wanted to raise at the board table, and Catherine had never indicated that she found it strange Kelly knew so little about her family's organization.

"Now to the next order of business," Catherine announced, as the applause died away. "That is the distribution of what we've raised."

"With Chad gone, I should think Kelly would make those decisions," Trevor Holcomb said, smiling at her across the table. "After all, she does represent the Lockett family interests."

"But she's been quite open about the fact that she isn't interested in the day-to-day running of the foundation. Isn't that right, Kelly?"

Kelly shifted her attention to the speaker, Leon Clements, whose family had literally been founders of the state of Maryland. The Clements were as blue-blooded as they came, but the wealth that had once gone along with that distinguished history had evaporated.

The rumors surrounding its loss usually concerned both Leon's drinking and his penchant for bad investments. She had no way of knowing if either was accurate. All she knew was that for some reason Chad had chosen him for inclusion on the board.

''I believe the current staff is quite capable of seeing to those,'' she said.

She could sense the shift of attention that had begun almost before she agreed to Leon's assessment of her level of interest. Although they had been willing to have Chad's hand on the helm, many of the board viewed her as merely a figurehead. The token Lockett. And for most of her brief tenure she had been more than willing to accept that assignment.

''However,'' she added, raising her voice and bringing the eyes that had already begun to change their focus to Catherine back to her, ''I find that I am *very* interested in the decision of where the funds should be allocated.''

''Here, here,'' Bertha Reynolds said.

An old friend of her brother's and a tireless worker, Bertha's place on the board was assured by those attributes rather than by any financial backing she might provide. She lived off a small inheritance and the kindness of friends like Chad, who had always seen to it that she was included in as many social occasions as possible. She, too, had been a stalwart ally of Kelly's during the first difficult weeks.

''Then perhaps you'd like to make us aware of *your* priorities, Ms. Lockett,'' Leon said. There was an edge of sarcasm in the suggestion, which Kelly ignored.

''Eventually. I have a few questions first. And I appreciate your patience with what must seem to some of you to be my very slow learning curve with all this. As you know, I very willingly left these decisions to my brother.''

There were a few murmurs of sympathy or understanding, which she allowed to die down before she continued.

''Now that I've been forced to assume responsibility for the organization that bears our family's name, I'd like a clearer understanding of how things have been done in the past before any decisions are made about what we do this year.''

"Ask away," Catherine said agreeably. "I'm sure that if we don't know the answers, we can find them for you."

There were assenting nods from several people at the long table.

"In going through the records for the past five years, I discovered that the pattern of distribution has changed considerably since the beginnings of the foundation. At that time, all monies raised were evenly divided among the five charities my brother initially included in the Legacy. Last year that division shifted so that most of the money collected was directed to only one fund. A fund that had been added to the original ones. I'm curious as to why that change was made.''

There was a prolonged silence. As soon as she finished speaking, Kelly looked in turn at the people around the table.

A few met her eyes openly. A couple seemed occupied with thumbing through their records, perhaps looking for some confirmation of what she'd just said. Catherine Suttle, one well-shaped brow lifted in question or surprise, had quickly glanced toward Holcomb and then away again.

"The division of the money was entirely your brother's decision," Leon said. "We weren't made privy to his reasoning.''

"And none of you questioned the change?"

"We each bring an agenda to this table, Ms. Lockett. Most of us were involved in supporting our particular charities long before your brother took a hand in raising money for them. Individually, we've always tried to make a case for the funds we were most interested in. The final allocation was always up to him.''

"So you have no idea why one fund was favored last year at the expense of the others."

"An idea?" Leon mocked. "Of course, I do."

"Would you mind sharing it with me?"

"Some highly successful politicking on the part of its proponents."

"Are you aware of where the bulk of the money has been directed?"

"No. I simply made an assumption based on the fact that I knew it was no longer going to some of the others."

"And the rest of you?" Kelly asked, again scanning the faces around the table. "Were you aware of the shift in the allocations?"

"Only through the complaints we received," Bertha said bluntly.

Her eyes, behind the thick lenses of her old-fashioned, black-rimmed glasses, were bright and alert. She might be one of the older members of the board, but she seemed to have a clear grasp of what was at stake here.

"Complaints?"

"From charities who were no longer funded at the same level they had once been," Bertha clarified. "There were a lot of those after last year's allocations. I received a number of calls because things had been budgeted based on an expectation of continued funding. Expectations that weren't met."

"We all made recommendations," Catherine said. "Anyone on the board who wanted to speak had an opportunity to make their case for the group they favored, just as I hope we'll be allowed to do to you. The decision, as always, was ultimately Chad's."

"Did you go to him about the complaints?" Kelly asked Bertha, ignoring for the time being Catherine's explanation.

"I tried," the old woman said. "He wasn't interested in hearing them."

"Actually, I tried, too," Donaldson spoke up. "He told me that he had very good reasons for the decision."

"Did he share those with you?"

"He didn't offer, and I didn't ask. After all, this has always been Chad's baby. He didn't seem to want any interference in the way it was run."

Chad's baby. Chad's foundation. As much as she would have liked to find another explanation, apparently what had happened to the money it collected was also Chad's responsibility.

"I HAVE THE ADDRESS and phone number of the people we discussed."

Catherine had waited until after most of the other members of the board cleared the room before she'd approached Kelly to hold out a folded square of thick, cream-colored notepaper. The older woman hadn't become the ultimate Beltway insider by being indiscreet.

"And you're sure they're trustworthy?"

"Impeccable credentials, believe me."

"Thank you," Kelly said sincerely, taking the proffered sheet of paper.

"Something you want to talk about, my dear? I am a very good listener."

It was tempting to confide in Catherine. Kelly was beginning to wonder if she had lost the ability to evaluate any of this. It would be good to lay everything out for someone who had known Chad. Someone who would be more objective, perhaps, than she was. Someone trustworthy.

Of course, that's why she had the folded sheet of paper in her hand. Professional, discreet and totally objective. Not even Catherine could lay claim to all of those attributes.

"Maybe later," she hedged.

"Anytime," Catherine said. "I mean that. You call me day or night. Your brother was a good friend through the years. I owed him a few favors."

Taking her hand, the older woman leaned forward to put her cheek against Kelly's, enveloping her briefly in a cloud of Giorgio. The unexpected kindness made Kelly's eyes sting.

When Catherine straightened, she took her other hand as well, holding both of them tightly. "You've done a magnificent job these last few weeks. He would have been very proud of you. Of course, he always was. He said you had more sense than the rest of his relatives put together."

Kelly laughed, squeezing the thin, diamond-encrusted fingers in her own before she released them to turn and speak to Bertha, who had come up as they were talking.

The praise warmed her throughout the rest of her goodbyes. It was almost as if she could hear Chad's voice. As if those words had been a message from the grave.

Pretty melodramatic, she thought as she gathered up the folders she'd brought to the meeting to shove them back into her briefcase. Her brother had never intended to dump this into her lap. He of all people knew how much she avoided exactly the kinds of situations his death had forced on her. And until she could find a way to turn it over to someone more qualified to run the Legacy—

One day at a time, she reminded herself. One hour at a time. One task at a time. It was the mantra that had gotten her through the days and especially the long, sleepless nights since she had received the news that had changed her entire life.

And now she was about to make a call that might alter it to the same extent. Given what she had learned today and what had happened yesterday morning, she didn't have any other choice.

Chapter Seven

"Thank you for seeing me," Kelly said, settling into the leather chair to which she'd been directed.

It had taken three days for the head of the Phoenix to work her in. When he had, the appointment had been after hours.

"I'm glad my schedule made that possible," Griff Cabot said as he resumed his seat behind the massive mahogany desk that separated them. "Do you mind if I ask how you found out about the agency? We have a policy not to advertise, so I'm always interested in how our clients learn about our services."

"I made inquiries of some people I trust. The Phoenix was the name that came up as an investigative agency that was both very good…and very discreet."

"I'm flattered," he said, smiling at her. "I don't suppose you'd care to tell me from whom those recommendations came. I'd like to know which of our friends I should thank."

Kelly wasn't taken in by the polite request. The information Cabot had just solicited had nothing to do with a desire to thank anyone. From what she'd been told about the ex-CIA agent, he was probably trying to evaluate her based on her acquaintances in town. She couldn't see providing him with any more information than was absolutely necessary. And she could chalk that cynicism up to her recent encounter with John Edmonds. Actually, there was something about Cabot that reminded her of Edmonds.

The head of the Phoenix had been younger than she'd expected. And far better looking. Of course, considering to whom he was married, a woman very much in the public eye as a legal analyst for one of the networks, she probably shouldn't have been surprised by that.

"I won't name names, but I *can* tell you that one of them is a friend of your wife," she offered, watching for his reaction.

Claire Heywood didn't use her married name professionally, but during their first discussion Catherine had been quite informative about Ms. Heywood's husband *and* his credentials. That he was a retired assistant deputy director of the CIA had made Kelly believe Cabot would be an old and distinguished civil servant, someone who would handle the matter that had brought her here with discretion. She could only hope the latter impression would prove to be more accurate than the former had.

"Then I'll express my gratitude to Claire. Exactly what do you think the Phoenix can do for you, Ms. Lockett?"

"Two months ago my brother Chad died when the private plane he was flying disappeared off Cape Cod. You may remember the crash. There was…quite a bit of media coverage."

That was an understatement. The search and subsequent recovery of the Citation had occupied the national press for more than a week. Not only was Chad a member of a prominent family, he had also been a perennial favorite on the most-eligible-bachelor lists, an honor he had more than lived up to.

"May I offer my condolences on your loss?"

Cabot sounded sincere. At least there was nothing judgmental in his eyes, which were still fastened attentively on her face. She chose to ignore his expression of sympathy, however, steeling herself to go on.

"Although the report from the NTSB hasn't been handed down yet, and won't be for some time, the *unofficial* verdict, both in the media and in the minds of the public, is that the accident was the result of pilot error. Compounded, of course, by the prescription medication in my brother's system."

The tabloids had made much of that particular autopsy finding. Granted, the levels had been higher than the prescribed dosage, but the allergy remedy was one used by millions every day. It had rarely been linked to the kind of physiological reactions the press had attributed to it.

"Even good pilots make mistakes," Cabot said. "I assure you I have enough hours in the air to attest to that."

"I'm sure they do, but in this case…"

She hesitated, knowing that she was about to move out of the grieving-sister slot he'd assigned her and into the conspiracy-nut category. She could only hope that even if he refused to consider doing what she wanted him to, he would keep his mouth shut about what she was about to say.

"Chad wasn't a *good* pilot, Mr. Cabot. He was an excellent one. He never took unnecessary risks. Anyone who has ever flown with him will tell you that. The weather that night, although not perfect, shouldn't have been a factor. Chad was instrument rated. The plane had just been through a thorough maintenance inspection. There was no reason for it to go down. Certainly *not* pilot error."

"You believe something else caused your brother's accident," he suggested.

Again, neither his voice nor his expression indicated he

saw anything unusual about the fact that she didn't buy what the papers had said about Chad's death. Of course, expressing doubt about a client's sanity wouldn't be good for business, especially considering the caliber of clientele the Phoenix apparently dealt with. That assessment rested not only on Catherine's recommendation, but also on the luxurious offices the agency occupied.

"Yes, I do," she said, her mouth dry with the enormity of finally putting the unthinkable into words.

"And you want us to try and find out what really happened that night."

"I *know* what happened, Mr. Cabot. Someone murdered my brother. What I want *you* to do is find out who."

THE DOOR BEHIND Kelly opened as she began to outline the things that had led her to that conclusion. She expected the interruption would be from Cabot's secretary, bringing some kind of urgent message for her boss.

As she hesitated, his eyes lifted, focusing somewhere over her shoulder.

"It's all right," he said. "Come in."

Since his words fit into the scenario Kelly had been imagining, she was unprepared for her first glimpse of the man who approached Cabot's desk. She might have had some clue if the lush carpeting hadn't masked his footsteps.

"Miss Lockett, this is John Edmonds, one of our operatives."

It was only marginally comforting to realize that John seemed as surprised as she was. His dark eyes touched on her face long enough for her to read the shock within them.

Since she had discovered the theft of the disk, she'd been convinced that Edmonds had had something to do with Chad's death. She had even decided that the encounter with the teenage thugs must have been a setup, designed to accomplish exactly what it had: to get Edmonds into the house and into a position to download files from Chad's computer.

Now everything she thought she had known when she entered this office shifted and realigned itself, based on Cabot's introduction of John as a member of the Phoenix. What she'd been told about this organization and its leader made it virtually impossible that they could have had anything to do with Chad's death. If they hadn't, then why had Edmonds, apparently with Griff Cabot's complicity, arranged Saturday night's charade.

"Ms. Lockett," John said.

There was a guardedness in his eyes that made her wonder if Cabot knew what had happened between them. Although that might be comforting from her standpoint, it didn't speak well of Edmonds's relationship with his boss, causing another realignment in her thinking. Was it possible he was playing his own game? That he *was* working for the people who had arranged for the crash of her brother's plane?

"Is this some kind of joke?" she asked, breaking the contact between them in order to address her question to Cabot.

"A simple coincidence," John said, bringing her attention back to him.

There was something about his voice that resonated inside her body. A latent memory of how safe she'd felt in his arms? Or something more primitive?

She quickly rejected the idea that what she'd felt might be sheer physical reaction to being in the same room with the man who had so thoroughly made love to her. *Made love.* The phrase again mocked her attempt to downplay the significance of what had happened that night.

"A coincidence?" she repeated. "That you tricked me

into letting you into my brother's house so that you could download information from his computer? I don't see how there could be anything coincidental about that.''

She had the satisfaction of watching the impact of her accusation in his eyes. Apparently, he hadn't expected her to have discovered what he'd done.

"I don't have any idea what you're talking about."

"Are you denying you spent Saturday night with me?"

After a few seconds' hesitation, Edmonds said the only thing he could under the circumstances. "You know I did. But if information was downloaded from your brother's computer, I can assure you I didn't do it."

"You admit to being there, but you're saying that you *didn't* steal a disk from his desk, copy material onto it and then take it away with you."

"That's what I'm saying. If someone did that—"

"There *was* no one else," she interrupted. "And you know it."

The silence that followed her assertion stretched until the head of the agency broke it.

"Ms. Lockett came to the Phoenix because she believes someone murdered her brother."

"Murdered?" Edmonds sounded genuinely shocked by the idea.

By now Kelly had decided that whatever was going on here, she had made a mistake in coming to these people. It didn't matter how highly recommended they came. She knew she couldn't trust Edmonds; therefore, she couldn't trust the organization he worked for, either.

Whether Cabot had been in on his deception the night of the auction or not, these weren't people she wanted to depend on to help her find Chad's murderer. She picked up her purse and rose. As she did, the head of the Phoenix stood, too.

"If there's a charge for your time, Mr. Cabot, send me a bill. Mr. Edmonds has my address."

Her eyes met John's briefly as she turned and headed toward the door. She was halfway there when Cabot's voice stopped her.

"We received information that your brother might have been implicated in funding certain entities who are unfriendly to the United States."

It took a couple of seconds for that to penetrate her anger, so that her forward progress had continued to the point where she was reaching for the knob of the door. When the import of the words "entities unfriendly to the United States" entered her consciousness, her hand hesitated in midair.

She turned to face the two men, both of whom were standing exactly where they had been when she'd risen. She would have sworn there was compassion in Edmonds's eyes, and as for Cabot—

"What the hell is *that* supposed to mean?" she demanded.

"It means that your brother may have been involved in a plot to fund terrorism, Ms. Lockett. Why don't you sit back down so we can tell you what we know?"

"IT'S AN INTERESTING THEORY," Kelly said, after she'd listened to Cabot's explanation, "but like the pilot error story, no one who knew Chad would believe one word of it."

"Perhaps your brother didn't know what was going on."

Cabot had already admitted their information was at best incomplete. Since she knew Chad couldn't have been involved in something like the Phoenix's sources had indicated, Kelly didn't see any point in continuing the discussion.

As she'd listened to Cabot talk, she'd been far too aware

of the other man in the room. John had propped his hip on the edge of a library table, located slightly behind Cabot's desk. She couldn't decide if his choice of location, in her direct line of sight, had been deliberate or not, but his posture was an unwanted reminder of the scene in the bathroom that night. And of all it had led to.

He hadn't made any other contributions to the conversation, content to let his boss do the talking. The longer she listened to the scenario Cabot was presenting, the firmer had become her decision to take her suspicions about Chad's death to someone else.

The Phoenix was welcome to do as they wished with that supposed link between the Legacy and terrorism. She couldn't stop them in any case, and she was confident they would find nothing to implicate Chad in treason.

"There was very little about the operation of the foundation my brother wasn't aware of," she said, confident enough of Chad's innocence to admit that. "He created it, and he ran it personally. Very efficiently, I might add. He was extremely proud of the percentage of money raised that went to causes and not administration."

"Perhaps he believed the charities he funded were legitimate when they weren't."

"I suppose that's possible," she acknowledged, thinking of the group that had recently been placed under the Legacy umbrella. "But I assure you money was not donated in a vacuum. I can show you how carefully those organizations were monitored. Actually, since Mr. Edmonds raided my brother's computer, I'm sure you already have that information," Kelly said, again getting to her feet.

"It must have occurred to you that the two investigations may be related."

"*Two* investigations?"

"You believe your brother was murdered. Maybe that

was because he discovered exactly what our source has suggested about the Legacy funds.''

Was that possible? she wondered. It would certainly give a powerful motive for someone to want Chad out of the way.

''If he had,'' she said, ''Chad would have gone straight to the authorities.''

''Then what makes you believe he was murdered?''

John Edmonds had broken his silence to ask the one question for which she no longer had a convincing answer. From the first, she'd been unwilling to believe that any carelessness on Chad's part had been responsible for his death. He was, as she'd told Cabot, far too good a pilot. She had also been suspicious of that supposed overdose. Neither of those fit with what she knew about her brother.

Then she had discovered the shift in the distribution of the foundation's money and had encountered the animosity it had evoked among the members of the board. Finally, the actions of this man in copying Chad's records had solidified her growing suspicions about her brother's death.

Now she understood why Edmonds had done that. It was obvious he had not been the agent of some group interested in wresting control of the foundation from her brother's hands, but rather of this one, bent on tying Chad to terrorist activities.

''What I believe is no longer of any concern to you,'' she said, refusing to try to justify her instinct that something was wrong about her brother's death. What would be the point, since they didn't believe anything she'd said? ''I came here to hire you to investigate Chad's death. I now know that for you to do so would be a conflict of interest. You seem to have your minds made up that he was a traitor.''

"We haven't made up our minds about anything," Cabot said.

"Well, I have. And by the way, I'll be filing a report with the police about the theft of information from my brother's computer. I'm sure you have friends in the department who will take care of that for you, but I thought it only fair to give you warning."

"Thank you," Cabot said without a trace of sarcasm, although one dark brow had arched.

Despite the fact that she knew she would regret it, she couldn't resist a last glance at the man she had so foolishly trusted. His eyes were downcast. He seemed to be studying his hands, which were clasped together and resting on his thigh.

The sight of those long dark fingers lying relaxed against the fabric of his slacks was an unpleasant reminder of how skillfully they had caressed her body. A memory she didn't need or want right now.

No one attempted to stop her this time as she turned and crossed the room. She was determined at least to leave with dignity. Thankfully, she managed to hold her emotions in check until she'd pulled the door closed behind her.

She leaned against it to take a calming breath. Despite the thickness of its wood between them, she heard Cabot's voice from inside the office. "I had thought we understood each other. In no way could that be considered surveillance."

"Oh, my dear!" Cabot's secretary interrupted her eavesdropping, hurrying around the reception desk to confront her. "Are you all right? You're positively colorless."

Kelly pushed away from the door regretfully. It didn't appear John was going to escape unscathed from the interview with his boss, which couldn't have pleased her more.

She would have loved to hear the rest of what Cabot had to say.

"I'm fine," she said, smiling at the woman. "It's been a very long day."

"Wait until you're my age, dear. They're all long then. Go home and put your feet up. That's what I always do. Have a nice hot bath and a cup of tea. You'll forget all about your problems."

"It sounds tempting," Kelly agreed.

"Especially if you add a little bourbon to the tea," the older woman said, leaning close to whisper the last part of her prescription as if they were conspirators.

The real conspirators were on the other side of the door, Kelly thought, preparing to drag her brother's name through the mud more than it had been already. And there didn't seem to be anything she could do to stop them.

BY THE TIME she reached the car, she was shaking. She wasn't sure whether it was anger at Cabot's accusation or reaction to the realization of just how big a fool John Edmonds had made of her. Maybe a combination of both.

After she closed the car door, she sat for a long time without starting the engine. Holding the key to the Jag in her hand, she tried to think of someone to whom she could turn for advice. Someone she could confide in.

She realized that of all the people she had met since she'd been in Washington, there wasn't one she would feel comfortable relating her suspicions to. That's why she had sought out the Phoenix. She had felt it would be better to let someone professional handle her concerns. Now that had fallen through—

The unexpected knock on the glass beside her made her jump. She turned to find John, his hands on the roof, leaning down to look into the car.

"Lower the damn window," he demanded.

Instead, she inserted the key into the ignition, enjoying more than she usually did the responding growl of the engine.

"Get out of the way," she warned, shifting into reverse.

"We have to talk."

"No, we don't. Believe me, we've said everything that needs to be said."

"Did you ever consider that whoever killed your brother might have turned his attention toward you?"

For the first time since he'd entered Cabot's office, she turned, her lips slightly open in shock, to confront the man who had made love to her throughout that long night.

And who had then stolen out of her bed to search her brother's office while she slept.

Still, what he'd just said created a knot of anxiety in her chest. The idea might be ridiculous, but so was everything else that had happened. She rolled down the window, deciding that any further discussion on this subject might be better carried on at a reduced volume.

"What does that mean?"

"You didn't believe robbery was the motive for that attack in the parking deck. Neither did I. It made no sense that those kids didn't take the money. Not unless they'd been promised a lot more by someone else."

"And you think that means they wanted to *kill* me? That somebody *hired* them to kill me?" Her voice rose as she realized that was exactly what he was suggesting.

"I think, just as I did that night, there were too many things about that attack that didn't add up."

"Oh, they add up, all right. *If* you consider that neither robbery *nor* violence was the motive."

He shook his head. "What are you talking about?"

"If someone hired those kids so he could play hero. Congratulations, by the way. It worked. I thought I was too old to believe in fairy tales, but you had me fooled completely. Right up until I discovered you'd gone through my brother's files while I was asleep.''

He shook his head again, this time in negation. ''I told you. If someone took files from your house, it wasn't me.''

She wasn't buying his act. Not this time. Once burned, twice shy.

''And *I* told you there was no one else it could have been.''

''I didn't hire those boys, if that's what you're implying,'' he went on, as if he hadn't heard what she'd just said.

''Well, when you and Mr. Cabot find out who did, you be sure and let me know.''

She slammed her foot down on the accelerator, sending the Jag out of the parking space. He was forced to jump back as the car moved, but he followed, bending to speak to her through the still-open window as she shifted gears.

She didn't look at him as she pulled away, leaving a ridiculously satisfying trail of rubber behind her. And although she heard what he said, she didn't acknowledge it by so much as a backward glance.

''Watch your back,'' he'd warned.

Chapter Eight

There hadn't been many weeks in his life when things had gone downhill as rapidly as they had during this one, John thought as he unlocked the door of his apartment.

Sunday morning he had awakened in the bed of a woman who had intrigued him from the moment he'd seen her pictures in the research material Griff had given him. A woman who had come to his defense holding nothing more than a high-heeled sandal in her hand. A woman to whom he had later made love. She had even agreed to a future meeting, despite the fact that she'd obviously been having second thoughts about what had happened between them. Then this afternoon that same woman had driven away from him in a rage, accusing him of theft and deception.

The latter charge was valid, he admitted. Not in the way she thought, but in the fundamental nature of their relationship. He hadn't told her before they had become personally involved that he was part of an ongoing investigation of her brother. Now she would never believe what went on between them hadn't occurred because of the Phoenix's scrutiny of her family's charitable foundation.

That was only half of what had gone wrong, although it was the part that produced the most guilt, he acknowledged as he poured a generous shot of whiskey into a tumbler and drank it down straight. He thought about pouring another, but alcohol could only do so much to deaden this kind of failure.

Failure. That was the operative word. Especially professionally.

After all that time in Cabot's doghouse, he had at last been given an assignment that was potentially important. An investigation he could get his teeth into. One that seemed to indicate Cabot was finally going to let him off the hook for the incident involving Elizabeth and Rafe Sinclair.

This afternoon he not only had lost that assignment, he had lost his position with the Phoenix. Griff's comments had been both brief and scathing. *Spending the night with Ms. Lockett isn't surveillance. And since you failed to mention that you had in your report, you obviously realized that.*

He hadn't really taken time to dwell on what the loss of his job would mean to him. All he could think about on the drive home was the idea that had hit him as he'd listened to the conversation in Griff's office.

If there was the remotest possibility that someone *had* murdered Chad Lockett—and he hadn't been convinced of that by anything Kelly had said—then the anomalies he'd noticed in those punks' behavior Saturday night became more striking. And the warning he'd shouted as Kelly had pulled away this afternoon more necessary.

He could tell by her face that she had discounted everything he'd said. She'd made up her mind that he had tricked her in order to get into the house and steal the information from her brother's computer.

His hands paused in their automatic motion of unfastening the buttons of his shirt as he thought about that theft.

If information *had* been taken, as Kelly asserted, that meant *someone* had access to the house.

That's why she had suspected him. Because he'd been there. Inside the house.

Except he hadn't been the one who had downloaded those files. Given the reason she'd invited him in, searching the house while she slept would have taken advantage of a situation neither of them had created.

As far as Griff was concerned that consideration had been made moot when he'd accepted Kelly's invitation to come in. It was certainly moot now. What he did was no longer of any concern to the head of the Phoenix. Cabot had made that clear this afternoon.

That didn't mean, however, that he couldn't still look into whatever was going on around Kelly Lockett. Not that she would welcome his help.

The image of her attempting to come to his aid in that dark parking lot demanded that he not desert her. Until he figured out whether or not she was really in danger, he wasn't going to leave her unprotected.

KELLY HAD DRIVEN aimlessly for a couple of hours, every word that had been spoken in Griff Cabot's office replaying against a backdrop of unwanted images from the night of the auction. The headlights of the SUV appearing at the top of the ramp at the opportune moment. Her first glimpse of the man who had come to her rescue silhouetted in front of them. The sights and sounds of his struggle with the teenagers.

Those were always followed by memories of the events that had come later. The bruises on his face and body. Her attempt to treat the gash above his eye. His mouth slowly lowering to cover hers. His lips trailing over her body.

As always, when she reached that point, she blocked

those remembrances, deliberately returning to the scene this afternoon in the offices of the Phoenix. Back to Cabot's assertion about her brother's involvement in terrorism and John's denial that he'd downloaded information, neither of which she was willing to accept. They didn't make sense, not in conjunction with what she knew about Chad or with her discovery of the missing disk.

After that fruitless cycle, she always ended at the same point—Cabot's words. *I thought we understood each other. In no way could that be considered surveillance.*

Exactly which part of what John Edmonds had done had not been in accordance with his boss's instructions. The deception? The theft? Or her seduction?

Eventually she had given up trying to figure it out. Through the heavy downpour of a late-summer thunderstorm, she had finally directed the Jag onto the familiar streets that would lead back to Chad's house. To another sleepless night, she thought, unwillingly remembering the unaccustomed feeling of security when, for the first time since she'd been in Washington, she hadn't slept there alone.

She unlocked the door that led into the house from the garage, reaching inside to press the light switch as soon as the latch clicked open. She closed it behind her, taking time to fasten both locks before she punched in the security code that would reset the alarms. She was once more safe and secure inside Chad's fortress.

So why the hell don't I feel safe? she wondered as she walked down the utility hallway to the kitchen.

Watch your back, John Edmonds had warned. She hadn't done that the night of the auction and look where it had gotten her.

Not sleeping alone, at least.

Sleeping with the enemy instead.

Or was he? He had denied everything she'd accused him of.

Of course, he would. Especially after you mentioned filing a report with the police.

She hadn't carried out that threat, and she had fully intended to. It seemed the only recourse she had to what they were trying to do.

She changed directions, heading for the nearest phone, which was located in Chad's office. As she did, she remembered that it was John who had advised her not to report the previous attack to the police. If he had instigated it, then he certainly wouldn't want them notified.

She had fallen for everything he'd told her, she realized in self-disgust as she turned on the light in the study and located the phone book in the desk drawer. She flipped through until she found the listing for the D.C. police. She had already picked up the phone before she realized that she needed to decide what she was going to tell them before she dialed.

I let a strange man into my house and then into my bed. After we made love, he downloaded some files from my computer, and I want you to arrest him.

They would tell her she was lucky he hadn't cut her throat. She was. She couldn't believe she had been so stupid. Gullible. Trusting.

That was what hurt the most. The crux of her self-recrimination. She had trusted him. Completely. Instinctively.

And she had been wrong. So how the hell was she supposed to know who she could trust with what was happening within the foundation?

She put the receiver down. Her hand lifted away from it, hesitating over the box of disks. Eventually her fingers lowered, pushing the stack toward the back so she could be sure she was seeing all of them.

There was still only a single red one. Her sole evidence, in case the cops asked, for the assertion that someone had copied files from the computer. And admittedly, it was pretty flimsy.

She knew what they'd say. Maybe she'd used the missing disk earlier in the week. Or maybe there had only been one red in there before. And whatever she told them, John Edmonds was going to deny that he'd done this.

They might even believe him. This afternoon in Griff's office his denial had sounded absolutely sincere. Just as had everything he'd said that night, she reminded herself.

Sounding sincere was obviously part of his stock-in-trade. He had it down to an art.

That doesn't mean you have to be stupid enough to ever be fooled by him again.

It also didn't mean she had to report her previous stupidity to the police. They weren't going to do anything about someone she had willingly let into her home downloading a few files from her computer. In the grand scheme of crime prevention in this city, that would fall very far down on their list of priorities.

Which was exactly what he had said about reporting the attack in the parking deck.

She opened the drawer, shoving the phone directory back inside it with more force than was necessary. She didn't have to decide this tonight. If she wanted to report what he'd done, she could call in the morning. After she'd had time to get some perspective.

She needed time to separate her feelings about his very personal betrayal from the act of copying the files. And time to figure out what impact filing a complaint with the police might have on the Phoenix's investigation of the foundation.

She flicked off the light in the office to walk down the long hall that led to the bedrooms, making another decision as she did. She wasn't going to sleep in the same bed she'd shared with that lying bastard. She would sleep in Chad's room tonight, instead.

When she reached the doorway to the hall bath, she stopped, looking at the place where she had discovered John that morning. The whirlpool was empty and silent. Her eyes lifted, finding its reflection in the glazed mirrors overhead.

A hot bath and a cup of tea, and you'll forget all your problems.

If only it were that easy, she thought, dreading the long, empty night that stretched ahead. Of course, that hadn't been the only remedy Cabot's secretary had mentioned.

Bourbon was one sleep aid she hadn't tried. And if ever she had reason to resort to something—

Bourbon and a bath, she decided. A prescription that was far more appealing, especially tonight, than hot tea.

SHE HAD LIT the candles that had been artistically arranged by the decorator at various places around the bathroom before she'd turned off the overhead light and climbed into the whirlpool. Maybe the fragrance of the scented wax and the water would provide relief from the stresses of the day, even if the storm that had driven her home still raged outside.

She leaned back, resting her head against the same cushion where John Edmonds's dark one had rested. Remembering the scene, she looked up at the mirrored tiles on the ceiling.

Her eyes tracked across them to the open door to the

hall. To the exact place where she had stood that morning. Watching him. So sure he was unaware of her presence.

After a few seconds she pulled her gaze away to study her own reflection in the mirrors overhead. The water hid her body—just as it had hidden his, except for the contusions and abrasions on his chest and shoulders.

Self-inflicted injuries?

She had accused him of that. In thinking back on the fight, however, she couldn't pinpoint a single instance that seemed staged or fake.

And a lot of people believe televised wrestling is real.

Disgusted with her endless preoccupation with Edmonds and what he'd done, she sat up, pursing her lips. The breath she released was strong enough to flutter strands of hair that had escaped from the loose knot on the top of her head. She'd been over and over this, and she was getting nowhere.

Because there's nowhere to go with it. You slept with the wrong guy. You aren't the first woman to do that, and you won't be the last. It's time to let it go.

She reached for the glass of bourbon sitting on the edge of the tub and brought it to her lips to take a long swallow. She grimaced at the taste, but the burn as it made its way to the bottom of her stomach was comforting.

As she set the tumbler back on the rim, there was a noise from somewhere in the back of the house. Although very faint, it had sounded like something breaking. Maybe glass or—

Breaking glass?

She froze, listening so hard now that she didn't dare to breathe.

There was nothing. No other sound. Only the steady drumming of the rain and the occasional low rumble of thunder.

A product of an overwrought imagination, she decided.

Or something that had a perfectly logical explanation. Something blown over by the storm. A neighbor's garbage can, maybe.

Except today wasn't garbage day.

Watch your back, John had warned.

In one noisy motion, she pushed up out of the whirlpool, grabbing the bath sheet she had tossed on the bench beside it. She hadn't even brought a robe into the room.

The clothes she had worn were scattered on the floor and the counter, lying where she had discarded them as she'd undressed. Ignoring them as too difficult to don while she was wet, she wrapped the towel around her body sarong-style as she crossed the room.

Despite the fact that she was barefoot, she tiptoed, leaving wet half footprints on the black marble. She stopped to listen when she reached the door.

The silence in the house seemed thick. Almost threatening. The hair on the back of her neck began to lift as it had that night in the dark parking deck.

If the sound she'd heard had been someone breaking a window to get in, why the hell hadn't the alarm gone off?

Or maybe it had. Maybe it sounded at the police station or at the offices of the security company.

She couldn't believe she didn't know, but learning all the bells and whistles of Chad's many gadgets hadn't been high on her list of priorities. There had been too many other things to do in the time she'd spent here.

She needed to get to a phone and call the cops, she decided. Let them sort it out when they got here—even if what she'd heard had only been the neighbor's garbage cans clanging.

Just make the call. It's what they get paid to do. They're used to hysterical women.

The nearest phone was in Chad's bedroom. She took the final step that put her in the middle of the open doorway.

Once there, she leaned forward enough to see out into the hallway. It was completely dark, except for a dim light at the front of the house, which looked as if it might be coming from the streetlights outside.

Phone.

She sprinted toward the end of the hall where the master suite was located. She entered the room at a run, her feet soundless as she flew across the carpet.

She reached the bedside table, grabbing the receiver off the stand and immediately turning to face the door. Then, her back to the wall, she slid down until she was concealed by the shadows.

She punched in 911 with trembling fingers and then put the phone up to her ear. It took a second or two for the lack of sound to register.

When it did, she held the receiver away from her, looking down at it to push the talk button off and then on again. When she lifted the phone to her ear once more, it was still dead.

The storm must have knocked out the power. She couldn't bear to think of the alternative. That someone had cut the line, deliberately isolating her from help.

John Edmonds?

Had he arranged this stunt so he could mount another fake rescue. Or to make her take his warning seriously? Or could this be another attempt by the Phoenix to find something in the house that they could use to convict her brother of treason? Of course, he *had* denied that he'd downloaded the information to try to do that.

Yeah, you son of a bitch. It was all those other men I let into the house who did it.

If someone was in the house, however…

Did you ever consider that whoever killed your brother might now have turned his attention toward you?

She swallowed against the growing ache in her throat. Reaching out, she placed the useless receiver back on the cradle, careful not to make any noise as she did.

She had no idea if Chad's elaborate alarm system would work with the phone lines disabled. And she couldn't remember where she had left her purse with her cell phone.

She tried to visualize her progress through the house to jog her memory about where she had laid down her purse and briefcase. Probably when she had gone into Chad's office to look up the number of the police department.

She hadn't had either of them in her hands when she'd taken the top off the decanter on the bar there. The mental picture of that action was suddenly piercing in its clarity. She had laid the crystal stopper on the bar as she'd filled the Old Fashion glass to carry with her into the bathroom. And she couldn't remember putting it back on top of the bourbon.

Could that possibly have been what she'd heard? The sound of the stopper rolling off and smashing on the hardwood floor?

If it *had* rolled off, would it have broken, given its thickness? Would it have been loud enough for her to hear it over the sound of the rain? Was she cowering in here because she'd been careless with the family crystal?

Son of a bitch.

He had done this to her. She had never been afraid here before. Not once in all those nights when she hadn't been able to sleep. Not once.

Now she was hiding naked in the bedroom because she'd heard a noise. All because some bastard had set her up as a patsy.

And then set her up again by warning her that someone was out to kill her. That was ludicrous.

And so was this.

Putting her hand on the top of the bedside table, she pushed herself to her feet. She was again conscious that she was wearing only a towel, but there was nothing in here she could put on.

She had cleaned Chad's things out of the drawers and closets during the first month she'd lived in the house. She had started the task one night when she couldn't sleep, working through the long, dark hours in a fit of rage that someone who had been so alive was gone. Angry that he would never wear those beautiful, expensive clothes again. Would never again live in the house he had loved.

Banishing that memory, she moved across the thick carpet, gaining confidence with every step. She'd been tired, a little buzzed with the unaccustomed liquor, and she had overreacted to some harmless noise. That didn't mean she had to continue to make a fool of herself.

She started down the hall, every sense alert, despite her determination not to let her imagination run away with her again. As she passed by the open door of the bathroom, she glanced in, the gesture unthinking.

The Old Fashion glass that contained her half-finished drink was sitting where she had left it on the rim of the tub. The candles still flickered, giving the black marble an eerie, almost spectral glow.

Automatically her eyes lifted to focus once more on the mirrored tiles, just as they had when she'd first come into the house tonight. The candle flames were reflected there, small beacons of light within the storm-created darkness that surrounded her.

She had already lifted her foot to take the next step when she became aware that there was something in the reflection that shouldn't have been there. There was a shape within the huge glass shower enclosure that she was sure hadn't been there before. As she tried to make sense of what she was seeing, whatever it was began to move, the amorphous shadows defining themselves into a man.

He must have noticed movement in the glass above his head. At that instant he looked up, the eye holes in the black ski mask he wore revealing soulless dark eyes, which met hers in the overhead mirror.

Chapter Nine

What he was doing tonight would certainly meet Griff's definition of surveillance, John thought in bitter amusement. And if it weren't for the intensity of the storm, he might even be able to see the house he was watching.

He leaned back in the seat, stretching the cramped muscles in his back. The aches and pains from Saturday night's attack hadn't completely disappeared, and the aspirin he'd taken earlier was wearing off. He thought longingly about that big whirlpool inside the house.

He glanced down at his watch, trying to imagine what Kelly would be doing now. He had watched her arrival, wondering where she'd spent the hours since she'd left the Phoenix.

He hadn't gotten more than a glimpse of her because she'd pulled the Jag into the attached garage and entered the house through an interior door. Once she was inside, he'd been able to relax a little.

The alarm system was one thing he *had* checked out Sunday morning, mostly out of curiosity and because security systems were something he knew a lot about. This one was state-of-the-art, just as he would have expected someone like Chad Lockett to have.

Which meant, he supposed, that there wasn't much point

in sitting out here in the rain. It was after ten, and she had put the car in the garage. That was almost certain to mean she wasn't going anywhere else tonight. Judging by how dark the house was, she might even have gone to bed.

Bed. For a moment the image of what had occurred between them replaced the surrounding darkness and the sound of the rain pounding against the roof of the SUV. That was something he couldn't afford to think about. If he did, he was going to be knocking on her door instead of doing what anybody with good sense would do at this point. Start the car and drive away.

He had no reason to be here. None that would stand up to official scrutiny if she noticed him parked out here and called the cops. And as angry as she'd been when she found out that he worked for the Phoenix, she would call them in a heartbeat.

It wouldn't matter that they'd made love most of that night. Or that she'd spent the rest of it curled against his side until pain had driven him to the whirlpool. Actually, that would probably give her added incentive to make that call.

It didn't keep him from remembering, however. The way she'd looked in that red dress. And out of it. The way she'd moved beneath him, answering every demand he'd made of her. Those unexpected tears.

Crying for her brother? he wondered as his fingers closed around the key, which he'd left in the ignition. Her loss was both recent and unexpected. The hardest kind to reconcile.

As far as he could remember from the material he'd been given, Chad had been her only close relative. There were some distant cousins, but he didn't think any of them even lived nearby.

That meant she had no family and few friends in Washington. And she was trying to assume control of a multi-million-dollar organization that might be involved in treasonous activities. As might her dead brother. It was no wonder she had cried.

Of course, most people would find it difficult to feel sorry for someone as privileged as Kelly Lockett. He was a little surprised that he did.

If she needed consoling, she could afford to hire someone, he thought with a lingering trace of bitterness as he turned the key in the ignition. After this afternoon, he knew that person sure as hell wouldn't be him.

BOTH HIS MOVEMENT and her identification of the shape as a man occupied the same split second. Her reaction to the thought of someone hiding in her shower was almost simultaneous, fueled by the adrenaline that had been flooding her system since she'd climbed out of the whirlpool.

Fight or Flight. And just as she had in the parking deck, she knew which it would have to be. She had one advantage. She knew the house.

Please, God, let me know it better than he does, she prayed as she ran.

She had only seconds before he would throw open the door to the shower and follow her. Seconds to find somewhere to hide within these rooms where he couldn't find her.

The power outage was now a blessing. The house was totally dark as she ran, the sounds of pursuit behind her.

The choices she made were instinctive, but always she could hear him. Occasionally she could even see the light from the flashlight he carried. Because of it she could tell that he had slowed to look for her in the rooms she passed. That added another few seconds' advantage to the slim one she had started with.

Kitchen, utility room and then garage. She formulated the plan as she ran.

An outside door there opened onto the back lawn. From it to the hedge and then into the apron of woods that edged the back of the houses and finally down to the creek bed at the bottom of the ravine.

Everything would be overgrown with the summer's heat. He'd never find her, not with the curtain of the storm to hide her movements. If she could only get out of the house before he caught up with her....

She skidded through the kitchen doorway, bare feet slapping as she ran across the ceramic tile. In the darkness she didn't see the metal garbage can before she bumped into it, sending it scraping loudly across the floor.

She used her hands on its top to regain her balance, sucking in her breath at the agony in the toe she'd stubbed. Ignoring the pain, she sidestepped the can, again heading for the back door.

As she passed the counter with the butcher-block knife rack, she thought briefly about grabbing one. Instead she sped by, acknowledging how useless it would be. She didn't know the first thing about using a knife. She *did* know that the kitchen variety wasn't the same as the kind people fought with. The kind that had guards.

And maybe it was like what they said about a gun. If you aren't willing to use it, don't own one. Someone will take it away from you and turn it against you, and the thought of a blade slicing into her skin—

The door to the utility room was suddenly in front of her. She slid to a stop, right hand turning the dead bolt while the left fumbled to release the chain. Her fingers were shaking so badly that she had trouble getting it out of the slot.

The sounds behind her grew louder. As did her breathing,

sobbing in and out as she struggled to free the stupid chain. She closed her mouth, sinking her teeth into her bottom lip to block the sound.

At last the knob at the end slipped out of the slot. She let go of the chain, which bounced against the frame as she pulled the door open. She prayed he wasn't near enough to hear.

Despite her panic, she took time to ease the door closed behind her. Leaving it open would be a dead giveaway of where she'd gone.

She ran past the washer and dryer and the upright freezer to the door that led into the garage. Dead bolts only, thank God. Again she took time to ease the door closed behind her.

Once she had, she stopped and listened again, her breath shuddering in and out in the silence. She could hear nothing. Either the utility hallway that ran between here and the kitchen insulated her from the sound of his pursuit, or she had lost him.

Maybe he was searching in the wrong direction. In the billiard room or toward the deck and the pool. *Please let him be anywhere but behind me.*

Acknowledging that he could be, she stepped off the single step and onto the cool, concrete floor of the garage. As she ran across it, she lapped the bath sheet more securely across her breasts.

The outer door, which was at the side of the garage rather than grouped at the front with the remote-controlled drive-through, had small panes of glass in the top half. Leaning forward, she resting her forehead against her arched fingers, peering into the darkness.

Nothing was visible but the curtain of rain, drumming with a renewed intensity on the roof of the garage. Louder here because there was less to absorb the sound. And once she was outside…

Her right hand fastened around the knob as her left turned the bolt. The door squeaked as she pulled it inward, then she stepped through it and out into the storm.

Squinting against the ferocity of the downpour, she looked toward the street. There were a few cars parked along it, but no lights on in any of the houses across the way. She used the back of her wrist to rub water from her eyes, trying to decide if there was even the faint glow of a candle inside any of them, which might indicate someone was home.

She couldn't be sure. Better the wooded darkness where there were places to hide than to chance crossing the open street to find empty houses and doors locked against her. As hard as it would be to be alone in the woods, at least she wouldn't be as exposed if she went toward the creek.

Through the hedge, and then along it until she reached trees. She could elude him there.

Suddenly there was a noise behind her. A door opening? Or maybe the same garbage can she had bumped again scraping across the kitchen tile?

Whatever it had been, the sound was all the impetus she needed to force her decision. She ran toward the hedge, which loomed tall and dark at the edge of the lawn.

Although it was intended to butt up to the decorative fence that backed the driveway, forming a barrier between Chad's lot and his neighbor's, there was a space between the foliage and the wood. She forced her way through the nearly nonexistent gap, twigs tearing the bare skin of her legs and chest. She was aware of their burn but far more focused on listening for further sounds from the house.

Once on the other side, she realized that if someone did what she had just done, he would be able to see her as she ran along the hedgerow to the woods. Torn again by in-decision, she glanced up at the nearest neighbor's house, between her position and the street.

It, too, was dark, but the foundation plantings, grown large with age, offered a dozen places for concealment. Right now they seemed more tempting than running through the woods barefoot and half-naked.

No time. *No time.*

She had to make a choice and stay with it. As she turned, taking the first step toward the sloping lawn that led to the creek and the woods, someone pushed through the gap be-tween the hedge and the fence.

She screamed, a startled shriek of sound, and tried to leap forward. Her attempt to flee was too little and far too late. In the darkness a hand closed around her wrist. And no matter how much she twisted and turned, she couldn't free it.

She raised her other hand, closed into a fist, and struck at the man's head. The blow landed ineffectually on his shoulder as he turned his body to avoid it.

It was only then that she realized he was no longer wear-ing the ski mask. As she brought her fist back to strike at him again, he turned to face her, squinting at her through the driving rain.

"What the hell's the matter with you?"

Edmonds. Despite her suspicions, she hadn't seriously believed he was the man hiding in her shower. Waiting for her to return to the candlelit whirlpool so he could kill her?

With that terrifying thought, she completed her swing, hitting him on the side of the head as hard as she could. His grip loosened as the blow connected. She heard his grunt of pain and felt nothing but a sense of satisfaction that she'd managed to hurt him.

He recovered far more quickly than she did. His fingers

tightened like a vise around her arm. He jerked her to him. Off balance, she fell against his chest, her eyes lifting to his face.

The gash above his eye had reopened, obviously the result of the blow she'd struck. Rainwater mingled with blood ran in rivulets down his cheek.

''Stop it,'' he demanded. His free hand gripped her bare shoulder, shaking her hard.

She tried to raise her fist to hit him again, but this time he caught her arm before she could complete the motion. Holding both her wrists, he pulled her to him again. His breathing was as ragged as hers, his features contorted with rage.

''What the hell are you doing out here?''

Within the fear that seemed to have paralyzed her brain, the words reverberated. *What the hell are you doing out here?* It was not the question of a man who had chased her from the house.

No mask. A white dress shirt, soaked by rain to near transparency. Her impression of the figure hiding in the shower, although fleeting, had been one of total darkness. Black mask. Black clothing. Was it possible—

He shook her again, harder this time. Demanding. ''What are you running from?''

''A man,'' she panted, having made the mental concession that the person she was running from had not been *this* man. ''He was hiding in the shower.''

Despite the hedge that blocked his view, his gaze returned to the house before it came back to her.

''You're sure?''

She nodded. ''I saw him in the mirror tiles on the ceiling.''

Through the rain that blurred her vision, she watched as understanding invaded his eyes.

"Come on," he ordered.

He released one wrist, pulling her toward the street with the other. He wasn't running, but the length of his stride made it impossible for her to keep up without doing so.

"Where?" she asked, resisting.

"Car," he threw over his shoulder.

He meant *his* car, she realized as they paralleled the driveway, passing the closed garage doors.

"What about *him?*"

"You call the cops?"

"The power's out."

"Then we call from the car and wait for them to arrive."

For some reason she had been expecting him to charge into the house to chase the guy in the mask. Which, given the unknowns, would be almost criminally stupid. A realization John had obviously made already.

The man might be armed. He might not be alone. And she had no idea where he was. Maybe he was no longer inside. Maybe he'd used another exit and had already made his escape.

Whatever the situation, John was right. At this point, with the two of them safely out of the house, this had become a matter for the police.

He opened the driver's side door of the SUV, pushing her in under the steering wheel and then following her immediately. As they fell together onto the split seats, the bath sheet got caught beneath their bodies. The fabric that had stayed securely wrapped across her chest during her frantic run pulled free, exposing her breasts.

He had continued to scramble in over her, his arm outstretched toward the glove compartment. He popped the catch, and his hand disappeared inside and then reappeared with a gun. A reassuringly large gun.

As soon as he'd secured it, he used the steering wheel

to pull himself upright. Eyes focused on the dark house, he shifted the gun to his left hand, fumbling for the cell phone that was apparently supposed to be in the center console.

Unable to find it in the welter of bare legs and wet toweling, he turned from his concentration on the house to locate it visually. His gaze touched briefly on her breasts before it lifted to her face. Their eyes met and held.

He was the one who broke the contact, raising the hip that held the fabric of the towel captive. She pulled it free, backpedaling across the passenger seat. As she did, she tugged the bath sheet up, trying to cover her breasts.

He didn't look at her again. Instead he found the phone and punched in numbers. She listened, breath ratcheting in and out, as he gave the dispatcher the information about the address and situation. His eyes never left the house.

By the time he finished, she was feeling less vulnerable. More secure. And she was forced to acknowledge that he was the sole reason for that.

"They're on the way," he said, putting the phone back into its holder.

She nodded, not sure what to say to him. Either he had saved her life twice or he was the world's biggest con artist. Warring with the latter supposition was the fact that he worked for Cabot, who had come highly recommended as a man of integrity and honor. It didn't seem he would sanction this kind of scam.

"Your eye's bleeding," she said.

As he had last night, he touched the gash with his fingers, and then held them out as if to verify the truth of what she'd told him.

"It's okay."

"You should have gotten stitches," she said inanely.

The silence stretched after that less-than-brilliant observation. After all, the cut had begun to heal before she'd opened it again.

"I'm sorry," she said softly. "I thought..." She let the sentence fade, reluctant to put into words exactly what she had been thinking.

"You thought I was the guy chasing you."

He didn't seem to understand that her belief he was the man in the ski mask wasn't just a matter of mistaken identity. She had thought he might somehow be involved from the moment she'd heard the sound of breaking glass. There was no way she wanted to try to explain that.

As they waited for the cops, rain thundering against the roof, it seemed more and more likely that she had been wrong. That she'd been ungrateful and distrusting of a man who had twice come to her defense when she had most needed his help.

"Thank you," she said.

Whatever else he'd done, whatever he and Cabot believed about Chad, she owed him. Big-time. She shivered, a combination of being soaked to the skin and the aftermath of the horror she had seen in those glazed mirrors.

He had taken his eyes off the house when she'd expressed her gratitude. After making another quick scan of the grounds, he reached into the back seat and held out the blazer he'd been wearing this afternoon.

She almost refused it, but she didn't seem to be able to stop trembling. She was cold and scared and more confused than she'd ever been in her life.

One hand still gripping the bath sheet, she reached out with the other to take the coat. Her fingers were shaking so violently their movement was visible.

He watched them fasten around the jacket, but he didn't release it. Her eyes rose to his, questioning.

He pulled the blazer away from her and then using both

hands, despite the handicap of the gun, held the coat up as if inviting her to put it on.

"Come here."

The words were low, but they were no less a command than when he'd ordered her to get into his car in the parking deck. She hesitated only a couple of heartbeats before she succumbed to the lure he offered.

She got to her knees, struggling to keep the towel over her breasts, in spite of its cold, clammy weight. As soon as she was upright, he wrapped his jacket around her, at the same time pulling her across the console and onto his lap.

Maybe it was insane, but she went into his arms willingly, huddling against the warmth of his body. Her head rested on his shoulder, the now-familiar smell of him surrounded her.

Soap or shampoo. Something clean. Clearly masculine. Far too reminiscent of the night he'd spent in her bed.

He had held her then as hot tears seeped from under her closed lids. Crying for Chad. For herself, too, she supposed. For all of it.

He hadn't asked her why she cried. He had simply held her. She had instinctively known then that no matter what happened, he was strong enough to keep her safe.

Just as she knew it now.

Chapter Ten

The cops had come and gone. Searching the house with their flashlights, they had found no evidence of an intruder. No signs of forced entry. Nothing to explain the sound of breaking glass she'd heard. It was as if she had imagined it all.

As their questions became more and more skeptical, she had almost begun to wonder if she had. There should at least have been a trail of muddy footprints leading into the house. She asked twice if they'd checked for them and been assured that they'd found nothing of that nature anywhere. There was not one thing in the house to indicate anyone had been inside it tonight except her.

She had been instructed to show them where she'd seen the man in the mask. As she stood in the doorway of the hall bath, the cops looking in over her shoulders, she realized that all the candles were still burning. Even her clothing lay where she'd left it. Everything was exactly the same as the last time she'd seen the room except for the presence of the man whose eyes had met hers in the overhead mirror.

John had remained silent during the interview, although he had certainly paid closer attention to her story than the officers had. They seemed to have a hard time following the chain of events, even after she had taken them physically through the sequence. The damp spot she'd left on the carpet beside the bedside table in her brother's room was still visible, but the cops seemed more interested in the accoutrements of the room itself.

The price of celebrity. They obviously had remembered the address from the mobs of sightseers and well-wishers who'd crowded the street during the search for Chad's plane.

When they finally ran out of questions, they had given her a business card with the precinct's number on it and told her to call if she thought of anything else. A matter of maybe an hour, if that, and they were gone, leaving her alone with the man she had suspected of having arranged the *last* attack on her. The one she had believed, up until tonight, had been a hoax.

"I didn't imagine him," she said to John, feeling a need to defend her sanity.

"I never thought you did."

"*They* thought it."

"Cops operate in a world of provable events. It's a necessity. They're required to see evidence and collect proof."

"And in this case there is none," she said flatly. She was having a hard time believing someone could break into her home and not leave any trace.

"*We*, however, can operate in a world of *probable* events," John went on. "Someone attacked you after the auction. Since they didn't succeed, it was always likely they would try again."

She said nothing, trying to reconcile his obvious concern with the anger she'd felt toward him all evening. He seemed to intuitively recognize her reluctance to trust him again. Or maybe that was more guilt than intuition.

"And I swear to you I didn't hire those kids," he said.

"You also didn't tell me you were working for the Phoenix."

"Because it wasn't relevant."

"It wasn't *relevant* that you were investigating my brother? That you think he was a terrorist. How could that *not* be relevant?"

"Because what happened between us—"

She waited, but when he didn't go on, eventually she prodded because she really needed to hear him say it.

"Because what happened between us…"

"It wasn't about your brother. Or the investigation."

She felt a nearly physical response to the strength of his assertion. "Then…exactly what was it about?"

"You know as well as I do."

"A grand passion," she mocked.

"That's as good a description as any."

"But not so apt perhaps as deception."

"Only about the investigation. And it was an omission rather than a deception."

"You can call it whatever you want, the end result is the same."

"And what's that?"

Memories I don't want. And a loss of faith in someone I trusted. That was the root of her anger. She had believed he was someone special. Someone who would put himself at risk for a stranger.

"Betrayal," she said aloud.

He nodded as if that made sense. As if he accepted her condemnation as justified. "You can't stay here tonight."

"What?" she asked, thrown by the change of subject.

Apparently he felt as if they had settled the question of what had happened the night they'd made love. He had betrayed her trust. He'd conceded that. Now it was time to move on.

''There's no power, for one thing. And the alarm doesn't work.''

''Because of the outage?'' Whether she stayed here or not, that was something she needed to understand.

''That wouldn't have affected the system.''

''Then why didn't it go off?''

''Because it was disarmed.''

''It was on when I got home. I reset it after I came in.''

''Then someone turned it off.''

That thought was almost as chilling as the remembrance of the ski-masked figure. In order for someone to shut off the system, they would have to know the codes. Thinking about that, she shook her head. Denying the possibility. Needing desperately to believe that denial.

''You have the codes changed after you moved in?'' he asked.

''No.'' She hadn't even thought about it.

''How about the locks?''

''There was no reason—''

''Then you have no idea who has been given keys to the house or information about the alarms.''

''Chad was very careful about that kind of thing.''

''Chad is also very dead.''

The reminder had been deliberately brutal, but she knew he was right. If someone Chad trusted had been ruthless enough to kill, they would be ruthless enough to do it again. Either for the same reasons for which they'd killed him or to prevent their guilt in his death from coming to light.

''After all, we *know* someone came into the house and downloaded information,'' he reminded her.

That was something else she had accused him of. She still didn't know whether or not to believe his denial. Perhaps her ambiguity about that was reflected in her face, prompting his next question.

"Don't we?"

We, however, can operate in a world of probable events.

"A disk was missing," she said. "That was the only thing I could think of to explain why it was gone. That someone had used it to download information and had then taken the disk away with them."

He didn't suggest that she could have been mistaken. She wasn't sure whether to be grateful he believed her or to take his willingness to believe as an indication of his guilt. Maybe he'd accepted her explanation so readily because he *knew* that's what had been done.

"But they didn't erase the originals?" he asked.

"I don't know," she admitted. She hadn't been able to make heads or tails of the complete financials and she'd made copies of most of Chad's data. It had never crossed her mind to check and see if the originals had been deleted.

"Then maybe we better find out," he suggested.

THE POLICE HAD GIVEN HER a few minutes to dress after they'd searched her bedroom. As she led the way to the office, she was conscious that she had on very little under the robe she'd thrown on. As strange as it seemed, the fact that John was someone who was intimately familiar with her body made her state of near undress more embarrassing.

"What did your brother keep on this computer?" he asked, settling into the chair in front of the monitor.

"A little bit of everything. His social calendar. Personal finances. The Legacy records."

"Official ones?" John asked as he called up a listing of the computer's files, an operation he accomplished with the ease of long familiarity. Of course, that shouldn't be surprising. Everybody used computers these days. Apparently even private investigators.

"Those were there, but the ones I always used were

Chad's. The money that was raised and where it went. They go back to the beginning of the organization.''

"He keep backups?"

"If he did, I never found them," she said before the significance of John's question hit her. "They aren't there?"

"On an admittedly cursory examination, there's nothing here that looks like financial records of any kind. And without backups…"

"I have mine," she offered. "That's how I knew a disk was missing."

His eyes lifted briefly from the material he was scrolling through on the screen. "How?"

She touched the box sitting beside the monitor. "When I was trying to figure out what the various Legacy charities had received this year, I used a different-colored disk to download the information about each fund. It helped me to keep track of them. There were two reds in here the last time I worked with those files. When I came in here that morning to get my briefcase, there was only one.''

"You're sure?

"That's how I'd known the allocation was so skewed."

"What does that mean?"

"When the Legacy was started, Chad chose five charities to benefit from whatever funds were raised. Up until about a year ago, the money was distributed fairly evenly among them.''

"What happened a year ago?"

"A new charity was added to the mix. It got the lion's share of the Legacy money.''

"What was it?"

She hesitated, feeling as she had in Cabot's office just before she announced that Chad had been murdered. As if she were about to do something irrevocable.

"An organization that's based here in Washington. You may have heard of it. Something called The Covenant."

His eyes widened, lifted again from the screen. "You know what The Covenant is?"

She hadn't, but she'd done some research after she'd discovered the reallocation of funds. The little information there was on the organization hadn't been easy to find. There was no media coverage of their activities because they chose to work behind the scenes. That lack of press didn't mean that they weren't influential, however. Anyone who had worked in Washington as long as John would know how powerful they were.

"The major supporter of the Annual Day of Prayer," she said. "And of the Christian Caucus. And a dozen other similar projects. I know who they are. I know what they do and how well they do it."

"Was your brother religious?"

"Not particularly."

"But he was funneling…what? A couple of million dollars to a group whose purpose is to exert a Judeo-Christian influence in this town?"

"This year's auction took in over eight million," she said, watching his eyes again react with surprise. "Under last year's formula, the major portion of that, over eighty percent, would go to The Covenant."

"*If* Chad were still alive," John said.

She nodded, realizing where he was going with this.

"And since he's not, what happens?"

"I decide what to do with the money. Guided by the advice of the board."

"Have they offered any?"

"A lot of it. All conflicting," she said. "They each have their own favorite among the original five charities. Usually it's something they were involved in before Chad tapped them for the board. Some of them have been pretty insistent that I change the current formula.''

"So you've talked to them individually?"

"Most of them. They've called, or they've cornered me before or after a board meeting.''

"Did you tell any of them what you told Griff this afternoon?"

It took her a second to realize what he meant. "That I thought Chad was murdered?''

He nodded.

"I didn't have any proof. Just this vague sense…''

She hesitated, unwilling to admit that the one thing that had solidified all her suspicions had been the notion that he'd copied files from Chad's computer. She didn't want him to discount her strong intuition that something about her brother's death was very wrong by admitting how little proof she had.

"Chad and I were extremely close. I knew him as well as anyone on earth. We talked almost every week. After he died, a lot of what I was being told, by the police and by his friends, even by people on the board, didn't add up with what I knew. That he was somehow destroying the Legacy by changing the funding formula. That he would take an overdose of medication and then take off. He was too good a pilot for that.''

"You didn't *specifically* mention your suspicions to anyone? Daniels maybe?''

She and Mark had talked about Chad's death. Mostly about how hard it was to believe he was gone. Comforting one another. It was likely that at some point she'd said to him that she didn't believe the crash was the result of pilot error. That was a long way from saying he was murdered, of course.

"Not in those terms," she said, trying to remember if she had used the word *murder* to anyone except Cabot. "I *did* tell Catherine that I needed a private investigator."

"Catherine?"

"Catherine Suttle. She's on the board. She knows everyone in this town. She's the one who gave me Cabot's name."

"Did you tell her why you needed an investigator?"

"I think I told her that I wanted some answers about Chad's death. The NTSB report won't be out for months. I never thought that asking someone to look into the accident might be dangerous. And even if I had…"

"You wouldn't have believed telling *her* was dangerous."

"She and Chad have been friends for years."

"How about the others on the board?"

"They were *all* his friends. At least…they had been."

"Until?"

"I don't know," she said, but she did. And finally she admitted it. "Until the funding changed."

"When your brother got involved with The Covenant."

"The strangest thing is that I don't think he was. I can't find any evidence of that. And believe me, I've looked."

"How about someone around him? Someone in a position to influence him?

"Not that I've discovered. Of course, they don't make their membership rolls available."

"Almost medieval," John said.

"What?"

"A secret religious organization operating in the heart of Washington, D.C. It always struck me as an anachronism."

"That's not something Chad would have been interested

in supporting,'' she said decisively. She knew that in her heart.

"Then we need to concentrate on figuring out why he did."

"IT'S NOTHING LIKE your brother's place," John apologized as he opened the door to his apartment.

There was no way he could afford something like that, and normally he wouldn't think twice about the contrast. He couldn't remember ever thinking about how someone else might view where or how he lived, much less worrying about it.

When he'd discovered this place, one of the major selling points was that the building was old, turn of the century or earlier. The rooms were large, with high ceilings, hardwood floors and woodwork, and fireplaces that worked. Trying to view it with her eyes made him realize that the features he loved might not compare well with the up-to-date luxury of the house where she'd been living.

"It's wonderful," she said, "but…it's not what I would have thought you'd choose."

"Why not?"

"I guess I thought all bachelors would like the same kinds of things Chad did."

"Do *you?*"

She turned to look at him, seeming surprised at the question. "Where I live is nothing like that."

"In Connecticut."

She nodded. "It's a restored farmhouse. Very simple."

"You live on a *farm?*" His surprise was evident in the question.

"It was once. Now it's a bed and breakfast."

That information was added to the other bits and pieces he'd gleaned about her. Her courage. Her love of her brother. And because she had loved him, her willingness to step into a situation that must have been fraught with emotional peril. One that was now fraught with the other kind as well.

"Where should I put my things?" she asked, again choosing to turn the subject away from the personal.

There wasn't much choice for her accommodation. There was only one bedroom, because he'd turned the other into an office. The couch in the living room was a sleeper, however. He'd already decided to let her have the bed and a door that closed in hopes she'd feel more comfortable with the situation.

As awkward as this was, it had been obvious she hadn't wanted to stay in her brother's house alone. And he hadn't offered to stay there with her for a variety of reasons.

As he'd told her, there was no way to know who had a key or knowledge about the alarms. Given that reality, there was no way he could guarantee her safety there. She'd suggested a hotel suite, but he was more comfortable providing security in a place he knew like the back of his hand.

They hadn't been followed. He'd made sure of that. The only thing left to worry about was her discomfort over their previous intimacy. There was not much he could do about that.

"The bedroom's through here," he said, picking up her overnight bag and carrying it across the room to the hall.

She trailed behind him until he opened the door, stepping aside to let her go into the room ahead of him. As she hesitated on the threshold, surveying the bedroom, he tried to see it with her eyes.

He wasn't particularly neat, but the maid had come today. He could see nothing in the room that should have caused her to hesitate. Nothing except the bed. And the memories it evoked.

Despite his determination to let her call the shots, the remembrance of the night they'd spent together created an aching pressure in his groin. Resolutely he again banished those images, fighting for control.

"There's a lock," he said.

She turned her head, looking up at him. "Thank you."

She stepped through the door, and he followed, walking over to put the bag on top of the coverlet.

"There's only one bath."

She nodded, but this time she didn't meet his eyes. Hers were focused instead on the windows.

"Fire escape, but it's not accessible from the ground. The windows are locked."

"You must think I'm a real coward, but… I keep thinking about that man in the shower. Maybe if I understood who or why…"

"I don't think you're a coward."

She nodded, and there was another of those uncomfortable silences. Maybe she wanted him out of here. Considering what being in a confined space with her and another bed was doing to him, he couldn't blame her.

"The bath is down the hall on the right," he said. He had already started toward the door when her question stopped him.

"I left a perfectly good glass of bourbon on the rim of the whirlpool. I don't suppose…"

"You want a nightcap?"

"I don't want to think. Not about him. And especially not about what he was doing there."

"I'm not sure I have enough bourbon for that," he said truthfully.

"I'm a cheap drunk," she said. "Why don't we try?"

Chapter Eleven

John came awake with a start, unsure what he'd just heard. Something enough out of place in the familiar night noises of the old building to bring him out of a sound sleep.

Before he sat up, his fingers closed over the Glock he'd taken to bed with him. As he scanned the room, he eased his left hand under the right for support. He couldn't see anything that would be cause for alarm. He turned, visually checking the chain on the door. It was still in place.

He eased up off the sleeper sofa, his weapon held out in front of him. On bare feet, he crossed the hardwood floor until he reached the entrance to the hallway. Once there he paused, listening for a repetition of whatever had awakened him, before he stepped around the corner.

The door to the bedroom where Kelly slept was open a crack. His eyes darted to the bathroom door farther down the hall. It was standing wide-open, the room dark, just as he'd left it when he'd gone to bed.

No way, he tried to reassure himself, as he moved sideways down the hall, keeping his back against the wall. There was no way anyone could have gotten into this apartment. Despite his confidence in his security, ice touched along his spine.

When he reached the spot directly opposite the entrance

to the bedroom, he waited another second or two, listening again. Then he took a running step across the hall, hitting the center of the door with the bare sole of his right foot. The kick knocked it wide, the momentum of his leap carrying him well into the room.

Adrenaline pumped through his bloodstream so strongly that everything seemed to be happening in slow motion. Moonlight filtered between the closed slats of the wooden blinds revealed an empty bed, its sheets rumpled. He pivoted in a careful arc, his eyes examining the perimeters of the room and finding nothing.

The only place left to check was inside the closet. There was no longer a need for stealth, given the noise of his entrance. He strode across the room and pulled the door open with his left hand. Although he made a pretense of pushing clothing aside, it had been obvious immediately that she wasn't hiding there.

Why the hell would she be hiding? He was letting the events of the past twenty-four hours spook him, just as they had spooked her. Still on guard, he crossed the room, hesitating again when he reached the door.

If there were nothing wrong, surely by now Kelly would have made her presence known. After all, she must have heard him kick open the bedroom door. So where was she?

He stepped into the hall, striding down it to check out the bathroom. It was also empty.

Only the other bedroom, which had become his office, remained to be searched on this side of the apartment. He needed to look in there, simply as a precaution, before he went back to check out the rest. And before he gave in to the panic that was beginning to claw its way into his chest.

The office door was closed, which was how he usually left it. He put his ear against the wood, his left hand fastening around the knob. Hearing nothing, he pushed the door inward.

He had apparently left the blinds open the last time he'd worked in here. The same moonlight that had dimly lit the bedroom seemed as bright as day after the darkness of the hall. He squinted against it until his eyes adjusted.

An unfamiliar shape in one corner of the room registered on his brain. He had already brought the Glock into firing position, holding it out in front of him in the traditional shooter's two-handed grip, before he realized it was Kelly.

Huddled against the wall, she now seemed to be trying to shrink back into it. Maybe that was in reaction to the muzzle of his weapon pointing at her, he realized belatedly.

He raised the barrel of the gun slightly, taking her out of the line of fire. Then he leveled it in order to complete a slow circular scan of the room. He found nothing threatening.

"What's wrong?" he asked. After he'd waited several seconds, he prodded again, "Kelly? Talk to me."

Alert for whatever had driven her to take refuge here, he took a step closer. Her eyes, dark pools in a face washed white by moonlight, followed his movement, looking up at him as if in fear.

He advanced another pace and then another. Finally, still trying to figure out what the hell was going on, he stooped to balance on the balls of his bare feet in front of her.

Moonlight revealed what he had not been able to see from across the room. Telltale trails of moisture glinted on her cheeks, reminding him of the tears he'd wiped away the night they'd made love.

"Did something happen?" he asked again.

Wordlessly she shook her head. She was holding one of the pillows from his bed between her chest and knees. With a flash of intuition, he knew it had been used to muffle the sound of her sobs. And that's why she'd retreated here. To get as far away as she could from where he was sleeping.

"You want to talk about it?" An inane question to which he already knew the answer.

Again there was a side-to-side movement of her head.

"Nothing's going to happen to you here, I promise."

"I know." The words were almost a whisper.

"You have a bad dream?"

The whole night had probably seemed like a bad dream. Maybe the entire two months since her brother's death.

"I hate to cry," she said.

She sniffed, lifting her hand to rub the back of it under her nose. There was something about the gesture that made her seem incredibly vulnerable. More human. Subject to the same fears and insecurities as everyone else, despite her wealth.

"You need to go on back to bed," he said, holding out his hand to help her up. "Try to get some sleep."

She didn't take his outstretched fingers. Instead she turned away from him, looking toward the windows. Her profile, chin slightly raised, was limned by the moonlight reflecting off the cream-colored wall behind her.

After a couple of seconds her lips parted, and she took a small, snubbing breath. "You go on. I'm okay. Really I am."

He thought about it, and then instead of doing as she'd requested, he eased down to sit beside her, leaning back against the wall. He stretched his legs, clad in the thread-bare jeans he'd chosen to sleep in for modesty's sake, out in front of him, crossing them at the ankle. Although he laid the gun on his thigh, his fingers were still loosely wrapped around its grip.

They sat in silence for a small eternity, both of them

looking at the windows. He listened as she controlled the aftermath of what had apparently been a real crying jag.

When she had finally regained control, she said, "I didn't have anyone but Chad. Not for a long time. Our parents died in an avalanche, climbing some stupid mountain in Italy. A ridiculous expedition for people with two children. They were too young and too beautiful to die. I don't think I ever forgave them."

"How old were you?"

He glanced at her as he asked, but her eyes were still focused on the window. At least she was talking to him.

"I was eight. Chad was fourteen. Too young to become a parent."

"Did he?"

"He tried. He always tried."

"It must have worked."

She turned to look at him then, eyes questioning.

"If he raised you, he did a good job."

"How would you know?"

"Because I'm an excellent judge of character," he said, smiling at her. When she didn't return the smile, he went on, enumerating the things he had learned about her during the last twenty-four hours, none of them from the dossier he'd been given. "I know that you don't shirk responsibilities, even when it's one you don't want. You could have let the board and the lawyers handle things here, but you didn't. I know you're smart and that you've got more guts than most men I know. And if you're going to fall apart, you don't do it until the danger's over. *And* you do it in private."

She said nothing, but her eyes held steady on his face.

"When people will let you," he added, trying the smile again and getting the same result.

"Why in the world would you say I have guts?" Her tone was serious. Interested.

"I said smart *and* have guts. You probably saved your own life tonight by getting out of the house without letting him find you. That took intelligence and courage."

"All it took was panic," she said. "Don't give me credit for that."

"Panic doesn't allow you to think. Running was instinctive, but running smart… That's intelligence."

"It wasn't guts."

"Then how about coming to my defense armed only with a sandal?"

She laughed, the sound slightly watery, but clearly laughter, which made him feel infinitely better.

"*That* was stupidity."

"Inventiveness. You can have my back anytime."

"What does that mean? 'Have your back.'" The laughter had faded to a smile.

"I've got your back. You've never heard that?"

"I don't think so."

"Street talk. When you're in a fight. It means I'm right behind you. I'm protecting you. I've got your back."

"I couldn't very well stand there and let you take on four hoodlums on my behalf and not do anything to try to help."

"Sure you could. A lot of people would have."

"And a lot of people would have driven by when they saw what was happening."

He said nothing, knowing she was too smart not to make the inevitable connection. She didn't disappoint him.

"Except you couldn't drive by. You weren't there by chance."

"I saw you leave the party."

"And you followed me." Almost an accusation.

"Let's say I left at the same time."

"Because I was the reason you were at the auction." A trace of bitterness colored that conclusion.

There was no use to deny the obvious. "Griff gave me the ticket along with the assignment. I was supposed to watch you from a distance."

"That's what he meant today."

"Griff?"

"I heard him from outside the door. 'In no way could that be considered surveillance.' You were supposed to stay in the background. No matter what."

"Griff wouldn't have expected me *not* to get involved in that situation in the parking deck."

"Then…" She stopped, obviously having realized what Cabot had made reference to. "You didn't tell him you'd gone home with me."

"What happened that night wasn't part of the assignment."

"Are you telling me you didn't *once* think how helpful it would be to get up close and personal with the sister of the man you were investigating."

"It crossed my mind," he admitted.

It had, but that had nothing to do with why he'd made love to her. And as he remembered it, she had been as responsible for what had happened between them as he had. Obviously, now wasn't the time to remind her of that.

She laughed again, the sound a harsh contrast to her laughter of only a few seconds ago. "I'll just bet it did."

"That wasn't why I stayed."

"That's right. I'd forgotten. It was all about passion, wasn't it?"

"You didn't seem averse to a little passion," he said, and watched her face change, as if he'd slapped her.

Why hadn't he kept his mouth shut, as had been his

original intent? It wasn't easy to listen to someone twist your motives, but that didn't mean it was all right to strike back. Especially when someone was already so beaten down.

"I'm sorry," he said. "That was uncalled for."

"A cheap shot? Below the belt? Did I get the terminology right this time?"

"Yes."

A beat of silence.

"You deny that making love to me was part of the plan."

"*None* of what happened was planned." It couldn't have been. He couldn't have imagined that outcome in his wildest dreams. "Griff would never condone anything like that."

"Spontaneous was okay, though?"

Spontaneous as in combustion. It was apt.

"I wasn't supposed to initiate contact," he said. "I overstepped the bounds of the assignment in several ways, and Griff didn't like it. It's as simple as that."

"'Initiate contact,' she mocked. "Is that what you told him you did?"

"*You* told him what I did."

"Not everything."

"Enough," he said tightly.

"You seem to have survived his displeasure."

It was the perfect opening to let her know that he was no longer with the Phoenix. The problem was he wasn't sure how she'd react.

"Didn't you?" she prodded.

There seemed to be a note of concern underlying the question. Or was that more wishful thinking?

"I always survive," he said. *Arrogant bastard.*

"Did the CIA teach you that?"

"I wasn't with the agency."

"Somehow I got the impression that all of Cabot's people had been."

"From Catherine Suttle?"

"I guess." A small crease formed between her brows as she thought about his question. "Obviously, she was wrong."

"Actually, I was the lone exception."

"Why?"

It was the same thing Griff had asked him. And Elizabeth Richards. He still didn't have a good answer for what had drawn him to the Phoenix. Or for what had kept him there these last few difficult months, trying to work himself back into Cabot's good graces.

"I liked what the Phoenix was trying to do. I thought it was important. To use the skills Cabot's agents had acquired through the years to help people. I wanted in on it."

"And they were willing to accept you? Even if you weren't CIA?"

There were a dozen things he could have said to that, all of them tinged with his current disappointment. And therefore better left unsaid.

"Eventually. They took some persuading."

"Were you hoping to up your stock with Cabot? Was that what that seduction scene was all about?"

There was enough truth in that to make him uncomfortable.

"How many times do you want to hear this?" he said. "What happened that night wasn't about the assignment."

"And tonight?"

Despite the ambiguous nature of the question, his body responded to all the possible connotations. There was a flutter of anticipation in his belly and a physical stirring lower down.

"Tonight?" He was careful to keep any hint of either from his voice.

"Coming in here. Sitting down. Talking to me. The concern. Was that what Cabot told you to do?"

"Cabot doesn't tell me what to do anymore."

The pause was longer this time. "Why not?"

"You heard him. He didn't like my kind of surveillance."

"Are you saying…he *fired* you?"

"I was already in his doghouse. That was just the final nail in the coffin."

"What did you do? To get in his doghouse, I mean."

"The same thing I did this time. I made a decision that went beyond the scope of what I'd been instructed to do."

"If you aren't working for Phoenix, then why were you outside the house tonight?"

"Because I never believed those kids acted on their own."

"So you were watching the house—"

"To make sure no one decided to try it again."

"And someone did." She was again looking at the windows. "You tried to warn me, and I didn't believe you."

"If it's any comfort, I didn't think they'd try again so soon. Someone's running scared."

"That would be me," she said, again turning to face him.

"I'm not going to let anything happen to you."

It was easy to make that kind of vague promise, but he knew that she needed his reassurance right now. She had dealt with enough traumas for the time being. Besides, he meant what he'd just said. As much as he'd ever meant anything in his life.

"If you aren't working for Cabot any longer, maybe you could work for me."

There was no reason on earth to be offended by the offer,

but he was. He hadn't asked her for money. He wouldn't have. He didn't want their relationship to be about that.

And he couldn't see himself in the role of her employee. His own brand of arrogance, maybe, but that's how he felt.

"I don't know anything about charities." Maybe she'd get the hint.

"I didn't mean work with the foundation. I meant to work for me personally."

Personally. It had been personal since last Saturday night. It still was.

That meant he didn't want her paying his salary. He had a few bucks laid aside. He'd manage until this was resolved. If he was right about the depth of the fear that was driving these attempts on her life, that would be sooner rather than later.

"As what?" he asked, keeping his tone neutral.

"Personal security. Bodyguard. You decide what you want to call it."

"I don't want to call it anything. It's a bad idea." He began to push up off the floor.

"Why?"

"I'm not doing this because I need a job."

"Then why are you doing it?" she asked, looking up at him.

He held his hand out to her once more. This time she put her fingers into his, allowing him to pull her to her feet.

"I told you," he said when she was standing in front of him. "I'm a sucker for a lady in distress."

"That's very commendable, but it doesn't mean you shouldn't be compensated."

As logical as the comment was, there was something about it that got under his skin. Maybe he just didn't like to think about the financial gap that separated them.

And what does that matter? It wasn't like they were going to have some kind of long-term relationship during which he would have to worry about who was paying for what. The reality was he didn't have a job, and she was offering him a salary for services she needed. It was as simple as that.

Except, for some reason, maybe nothing more than again being close enough to her that he could smell that expensive scent she wore, nothing about this seemed simple. He had slept with this woman in his arms. He had run his tongue over every silken centimeter of her body. He would play hell trying to think of her as his boss.

Of course, there was always the possibility that that wasn't what she had in mind. She *had* made that comment about wondering what tonight was about. Maybe she was remembering the night they'd spent together, just as he was. As soon as his brain formulated the question, he knew he'd regret it, but he asked anyway.

"What kind of compensation did you have in mind?"

And watched the recoil in her eyes.

"I assumed you might have some idea what salary those kinds of services command." Her voice was no longer relaxed.

"I should set my own price. Is that what you're suggesting?"

A long silence.

"I could research it, I suppose," she said finally, "but I'm willing to pay you whatever you believe it's worth."

"Whatever it's worth to keep you safe?"

"Put like that…" She hesitated, choosing not to finish the thought. "I *do* understand there is risk to you in what I'm asking."

"I'm not worried about that."

"Then what *are* you worried about? Obviously, there's *something* about the arrangement that bothers you."

He nodded, holding her eyes. Her head tilted slightly, questioning.

Moving deliberately, he reached around his back and slid the Glock into the waistband of his jeans. Then, hands free, he reached for her.

Her eyes widened as his fingers closed around her shoulders to pull her to him. She put her palms flat against his bare chest, maintaining a narrow space between their bodies.

"This *isn't* the kind of compensation I had in mind."

"I never thought it was."

"Then…?" She was looking up into his face, her eyes almost black in the moonlight.

"I'll do what I told you I'd do. I'll keep you safe. But I'm not for hire."

"That doesn't make any sense."

"Maybe not, but those are my terms."

"Why?"

"Because when I do *this,* I don't want you trying to fire me."

He bent his head, tilting it to align their mouths for the kiss. At the same time he lifted her toward him, ignoring the pressure of her hands against his chest. For a moment her lips remained set and unyielding under his. Then, unexpectedly, they opened to the demand of his tongue.

Her hands no longer tried to push him away. Instead, fingers turned outward, they slid downward, one on each side of his rib cage, caressing his skin.

His breath caught in his throat as her fingertips forced their way into the waistband of his jeans, nails scoring over his hipbones. The subtle stirring he had felt earlier turned into a full-fledged erection, straining against the worn fabric that constricted it.

He gathered her close, trying to fit her body to the aching

hardness of his. She melted against him, her breasts separated from his chest only by the sheer cotton nightgown she wore.

He wanted more than that. He wanted what they'd had that night. Bare skin sliding against bare skin.

His fingers knotted in the fabric on either side of her gown, preparing to remove the last impediment to the fulfillment of that desire. She stepped back quickly, her hands gripping his wrists to push them down.

"Don't."

Her breathing was uneven. He could hear it in the sudden silence that fell after the sharpness of that command.

"Don't," she said again, more softly this time.

He forced his fingers to release the cloth, taking his own step back, reluctantly putting more distance between them.

She crossed her arms over her breasts, a protective gesture, but she didn't look away from him this time.

"That isn't going to happen again."

"Because you didn't enjoy it?"

He knew the answer to that. She had left him in no doubt about how much she had enjoyed it.

"That night was…an aberration."

He laughed, attempting to run the edge of his forefinger along her cheekbone. She avoided the gesture by turning her head away.

"That isn't what they call it where I come from," he said, making sure she heard his amusement.

"An aberration for *me*. I don't do things like that."

"I'd never have guessed."

It sounded cruel, but right now he didn't care. He was fighting the inevitable anger of rejection, as well as some of its other, less-than-pleasant side effects.

"If you're going to do what we talked about," she said,

"I don't think it would be wise for us to be involved in that way."

"Why?"

It was obvious she had no answer to that. At least she didn't attempt to manufacture one.

"What happened between us shouldn't have happened. Whether you believe me or not, that kind of thing... I don't do that," she said again.

"Make love to strangers?" The sarcasm was deliberate.

"Yes."

"You just made...an exception for me."

"I explained to you why it happened."

"Loneliness? Relief? Gratitude?"

"Among other things. A *lot* of other things."

Despite his anger and disappointment, he acknowledged the reality of her claim. She'd had a hell of a lot thrown at her. And he didn't want her in his bed if the only emotion that put her there was the feeling that she owed him something.

"You let me know," he said, starting toward the door.

"Let you know?"

"When it isn't about gratitude. Or loneliness. Or an aberration. I'll be around."

He completed the motion he'd begun before her question had stopped him. He had thought maybe she'd call him back. He wanted her to.

She didn't, which was okay. She wasn't the only one who had standards. Maybe she *didn't* make love to strangers. Maybe that night *had* been an aberration.

For his part he couldn't ever remember begging a woman to go to bed with him. And he wasn't about to start with this one, no matter how much he wanted her.

Chapter Twelve

She awoke to sunlight and silence. It took her a couple of seconds to remember where she was and why she was here. Another couple to remember what had happened last night. Both the intruder and the confrontation with John.

Still, it was a far better awakening than the morning of the last night she'd spent with him. She didn't have any regrets to deal with. At least not of the same kind.

He must think she was the world's biggest hypocrite. She'd allowed him unlimited license a few days ago and then last night she had refused to let him touch her. The really frightening part was how tempted she had been to give in.

From the moment he'd kissed her, memories of that night had washed over her in a flood of need and desire. He'd made love to her in a way no one else ever had, seeming to know exactly what would please her even before she did. Last night she had wanted his touch with a desperation that had both surprised and frightened her.

Almost as tempting as the memory of his lovemaking was that she had known if she let him into her bed, she would be able to sleep, just as she had then. His arms wrapped around her, her cheek resting against the steady beat of his heart. Comforted by his shared warmth. Protected by his strength.

Instead of savoring that sense of security, she had tossed and turned, reliving each minute of the previous twenty-four hours. Every time she'd drifted off, she would be jerked awake by the nightmare image of those eyes, revealed by the holes in the ski mask, holding hers in the mirrored tiles.

She shivered, blocking that terrifying memory by throwing the sheet and coverlet off her legs and forcing herself to get out of bed. She dressed quickly, pulling on the slacks and cotton sweater she'd thrown into her case last night. She took time to brush her teeth and pull a quick comb through her hair, but decided to forgo makeup.

When she opened the door to the hall, she heard nothing, although she thought she smelled coffee. She raised her nose, scenting the air. She was right, which meant John was up. At least she wouldn't walk into the living room with him still asleep on the couch.

He wasn't in the kitchen, she discovered. After a brief search, she found everything she needed for her coffee. It was obvious by the location of the powdered creamer and the sugar that he drank his black. And obvious by the level in the pot that he'd already had at least a couple of cups this morning.

Maybe he'd gone out, she thought as she wandered back to the living room. The sofa bed had been folded away, all traces of where he'd spent the night neatly hidden.

Or maybe he was in the office, working on the material she'd downloaded from Chad's computer. She was reluctant to put that hypothesis to the test. Of all the areas of the apartment, that would be the most difficult in which to face him.

Facing him anywhere was going to be hard enough after

last night. It was something that had to be done, however. She was only delaying the inevitable.

She tapped on the door, steeling herself for what was certain to be a momentary awkwardness. When he gave permission, she entered to find him working at a computer system that, seen in the light of day, appeared to rival her brother's.

"The locksmith is coming at eleven to change the locks at your brother's house," he said. Without looking at her, he pushed a sheet of paper that was lying on the desk in her general direction. "The security codes have already been redone."

"Thank you," she said, ignoring the paper.

Even from here she could tell that on the screen were the same numbers she had pored over during the last couple of weeks. The same churning sickness she'd felt every time she opened those files stirred again.

"I want to meet your board," he went on, not seeming to notice her distraction. "Can you arrange that?"

"I prefer not to think of them as *my* board."

He turned at that, looking at her over his shoulder. "That bad?"

"Some of them." She walked over to stand beside his chair. She was aware that his eyes had followed her, but she kept hers on the computer screen. "I shouldn't blame them. They're only fighting for what they believe is right. It's just that listening to them squabble about the funding—"

…makes me doubt Chad.

The words had been on the tip of her tongue almost before she'd even realized they were in her head. Up until this moment, she had never consciously admitted that she had any doubts at all about her brother's innocence.

She blinked, pulling her eyes from their focus on those

columns of figures. Only then did she realize that John was looking at her, his expression questioning.

"Listening to them…?" he repeated patiently.

"Makes me angry." She supplied a completion to her sentence that was the truth, just nowhere near the whole truth.

"Any of them lobby on behalf of The Covenant?"

"No. Most of them lobbied for something else. Which meant they were lobbying against it, I guess."

"So *they* aren't the ones who directed the money there."

"They claim the allocation was always Chad's decision."

"You have some reason to doubt that?"

Only my refusal to believe anything bad about my brother.

Of course, shifting funds around didn't mean Chad had done anything dishonorable. That had never been implied by any member of the board. That he might be involved in terrorism had been solely the suggestion of the Phoenix.

"What happens if you find something?" she asked, tilting her chin in the direction of the numbers on the screen.

"Something incriminating?"

"Something like what Cabot was suggesting. What he sent you to find."

"I report it to him."

There had been no hesitation in his answer. And no doubt in the dark eyes of the man who had given it.

"You aren't working for Cabot anymore," she reminded him.

There was no change of expression. No defense or explanation for what he'd just said.

"Or is *that* why you didn't want to work for me?" she asked. "Because your goals haven't changed?"

"I only have one. And it hasn't changed. To accomplish

it, however, I have to understand why someone would want to attack you.''

He had told her he would protect her. And she believed he could. The real question was whether she wanted his expertise at the cost of her brother's reputation and the destruction of everything he had created.

She couldn't have it both ways, she realized suddenly. She couldn't profess to believe Chad wouldn't have anything to do with funding terrorism and then refuse to have the organization he'd run investigated.

"It seems to me," John went on, "that if you believe your brother's death is related to the operation of the Legacy—and I *do* believe that, since the attacks seem to have transferred to you—then there are only two avenues to investigate.''

"And those are?''

"Either someone believed Chad was going to give the bulk of the money to The Covenant again or someone believed he wasn't.''

The first was the assumption she had made. The bitterness of the board members and their anger about the charities that hadn't been properly funded had pointed her to that possibility.

"You're saying that if someone killed him, it was either to keep the money from going to The Covenant—''

"Or that somehow someone with The Covenant had found out it wasn't coming,'' he finished for her.

A secret organization, which collected large sums of money that were virtually untraceable. They didn't claim tax-exempt status. They didn't have to account for where their funding came from or where it went. At least not all of it.

If Chad had for some reason become suspicious of their motives and mentioned to the wrong person that he no longer planned to donate the proceeds from this year's benefit, the largest in the history of the organization, then the scenario John was suggesting was as feasible as the one she'd imagined.

"We have to consider both possibilities," John said. "The members of the board, with their agendas. The charities themselves, especially The Covenant, since it was the wild card. The one thing that changed last year. And we have to consider your brother's relationship to each of them," he added softly.

She couldn't ask for one without allowing the other. She would simply have to trust that Chad was the man she had always believed him to be.

"Then what are we waiting for?" she asked.

"THE STRONGEST VOICES," John suggested, glancing away from the computer screen.

He had input the information she'd already provided him, which included a list of the ex-officio members of the board. Those were the figureheads, chosen for the cachet their names on the letterhead and their signatures on the fund-raising letters would give.

Chad himself had provided the glamour. And he'd been instrumental in convincing some of the capital's most distinguished citizens, including a former vice president, to lend their names, if not their efforts, to his cause. She couldn't imagine how John planned to use that information or why he thought it was important, but she had supplied what he'd asked her for.

Now they were coming to the heart of the organization, the people who literally controlled its fund-raising efforts. And she understood that every casual word she spoke about these people had the potential to lead him in the wrong direction.

"Hugh Donaldson. His firm handles the accounting."

"And he's a board member?" John's surprise was obvious.

"Is that unusual?"

"Maybe not for something like the Legacy, but, yeah, normally it would be."

She was perched on a bar stool he'd brought in from the kitchen and placed at the end of the desk where he was working. As his fingers moved over the keys, she had the opportunity to study his profile.

The bridge of his nose was slightly uneven, as if it had been broken sometime in the past. He had mentioned having a military background, so maybe it had happened then. Of course, it could just as easily have been some kind of sports injury. The muscles she'd felt under her palms last night indicated a long familiarity with physical activities, as did the breadth of his shoulders.

"I never thought about it," she admitted. "It seemed… I don't know. Convenient. Cost efficient. He was involved in the charities. Accounting is his area of expertise. Why shouldn't the foundation use his skills?"

"Conflict of interest, maybe." It hadn't been phrased as a question.

"Hugh doesn't benefit in any way from the funds the Legacy collects. He's not even compensated for the services his firm provides. He says it's his contribution."

"And undoubtedly he writes it off."

Of course he did. It made her feel stupid not to have realized that.

"So what's his hobby horse?" John asked, fingers poised over the keys.

"I beg your pardon."

"The charity he favors," he clarified, still without looking at her.

"Something called New Hope. It provides support for kids who've had run-ins with the law. Kids on the edge of more serious trouble."

"Why?" he asked as he typed in the name.

"Why does he help them?"

"Why is that his thing?"

She tried to remember what Chad had told her about these people through the years. She had realized almost as soon as this responsibility had been forced on her that she hadn't listened to her brother closely enough to gain the insights she so badly needed now.

"I think at one time he was one of those kids," she offered. "Look, I'm not sure I can tell you why everyone became involved in the projects they support. If that's important—"

"That's okay. Just give me your impressions. Everything else can be verified, but we need somewhere to start. How about his attitude toward The Covenant?"

Again she tried to remember and drew a blank. Hugh had been one of the less vocal members of the board concerning the controversy surrounding the change in the distribution of funds.

"I don't know that he has one. He just lobbied for more money for New Hope."

"No derogatory comments?"

"Not to me."

"Was anybody openly critical?"

"Of The Covenant? Or the distribution?"

"Either. Both."

"Leon Clements," she said. "He seemed angry about the way the decision was made."

"Angry at Chad?"

"Angry that he had been influenced. Maybe angry is too

strong a word. He was…caustic about the way things were done.''

"Who else has been *caustic?*" There had been a slight emphasis on her word choice.

"No one really. Not openly. Not to me."

"How about Catherine Suttle?"

"You don't honestly believe Catherine Suttle would have anything to do with terrorism?"

Or murder. Chad's murder. The idea was ridiculous.

"They aren't going to wear signs, you know. They're more effective that way."

He meant terrorists. And she knew that, of course.

"Don't patronize me." Despite what he thought, she wasn't a fool.

"Then don't make judgments about who couldn't be involved in what. Just tell me what you know about these people."

Controlling her anger, she took a breath and then released it upward, blowing a strand of hair away from her eyes.

"Catherine Suttle has been part of the Washington scene forever," she said, speaking slowly and distinctly, as if explaining something to a child. "She knows and is known to everyone, from the last three or four presidents to the current Senate pages she secured positions for. She's a Beltway native, one of the few people who grew up here."

"Daughter of the esteemed Senator Elijah Suttle."

John's tone was the same with which he'd reminded her of the tax implications of Donaldson's largess. In this case his mockery was also justified.

Elijah Suttle had been the quintessential career politician long before the term had been coined. It might have been invented to describe him.

He had served under a multitude of presidents and been

one of the most powerful voices in the Senate for over forty years. That heritage and her own potent charm had made Catherine the darling of those who had known her father, as well as the next two generations of Washingtonians who had only known *of* him.

"The *well-respected* daughter," she said. Whatever her father's reputation, Kelly had never heard anyone say a harsh word about Catherine.

"And a good friend of your brother's?"

"She's also been a good friend to me," she said, remembering the older woman's kindness, which had included providing her with Cabot's name and number. "Actually, she's been the most supportive member of the board."

"And of The Covenant maybe? In any case, whoever they are, she probably knows half of them."

"I don't doubt she does," Kelly said, "but she hasn't spoken on their behalf."

"So who does she speak for?"

"The Suttle Scholarships. Her only son was an artist. He died young. AIDS, I think, but she's never said much about his death. I think that's how she got involved in the arts. That and her background, of course."

"And despite the shift in distribution she remained supportive of Chad?"

"She was chairman of the auction this year. I think that speaks for her level of involvement."

"Which would mean she was in charge of security?"

"Ultimately, but details like that would have been delegated to someone on one of the subcommittees. All I can tell you is that with her in charge security wouldn't have been neglected. I think Catherine wrote the procedures manual on these functions. I meant to ask her at the meeting why there was no guard in the parking deck."

"Because they were only supposed to work until midnight," John said. "That's according to the contract."

"You've already checked."

"It seemed important."

It was, of course, but that didn't mean she would suspect Catherine because of it.

"Did the auction have a co-chair?" he asked, moving away from Catherine.

"Not a co-chair, but the next in command would be Trevor Holcomb, I guess. He's a lawyer. I'm not sure about the name of the firm, but he's a senior partner. His name's probably on the door."

"Silverberg, Holcomb, Sloan and Moss?" Without waiting for confirmation, John typed in the names as he reeled them off.

"That's it."

"Jewish?"

"I don't have any idea."

"Would security have fallen under his direction?"

"I don't know," she said again, feeling as if these were all things she *should* know.

"Holcomb have a favorite cause?"

"If he has, he hasn't been vocal about it."

"Okay. Is that everyone?"

"Bertha Reynolds," Kelly said. "Outspoken in the way only the elderly can get away with. Especially a small, birdlike elderly woman."

"Outspoken about what?"

"At the last board meeting it was about the change in distribution. She said she'd gotten a lot of complaints because people had been counting on the money for programs and hadn't received it."

"The charities had no warning they were about to be cut off?"

"Apparently not. They approached some of the board members, who in turn approached Chad."

"And he told them what?"

"That the decision had been made. And according to Hugh Donaldson, who also said he'd received complaints, by the way, that it had been made for very good reasons."

"Reasons which weren't shared."

"Not with him. Apparently Chad decided who got what. It hadn't been exactly the same from year to year. Judging by his records," she said, again inclining her head toward the computer, although the numbers no longer filled the screen, "he seemed to make the year's allocations by considering what the charities took in elsewhere. On who was likely to have a shortfall. On a wide variety of things."

"Your brother didn't offer anybody an explanation for why he'd gone against his own long-established precedent?"

"If he did, they didn't share it with me. And I asked."

"You get *any* explanation for the change?"

"Leon said it was politicking."

"Politicking from someone on the board?"

She mentally reviewed Clements's exact words. "He didn't limit it to board members. He just said someone had done some heavy politicking to affect the outcome."

"Then someone on the board, who isn't confessing to it, or someone on the outside."

"Someone from The Covenant?"

"The problem is no one knows who that might be."

"Obviously someone with quite a bit of influence over Chad," she said. "If I could see a list of names—"

"Medieval. I meant that in the most literal sense of the word. A secret society. Quasi-religious. No one knows who belongs or who doesn't."

"Why?" She would have thought that in the computer age, that kind of stuff could no longer be kept secret.

"Self-protection, maybe. An unwillingness to be labeled as religious. The founders didn't want the organization to be used to further the political ambitions of those who wanted to *profess* devoutness without actually being devout."

"So if no one knows who belongs, then no one can use their membership as propaganda to their constituents."

"Pray only in your closet. And don't let the right hand know what the left is doing."

"Secret contributions."

"Which are not tax deductible. You give because you want to. Not for what you get out of it."

"That's…"

"Arcane?" he suggested as she searched for a word.

"Who would contribute under those terms?"

"People who don't need a tax break. People who don't want to make hay, political or otherwise, out of their deeply held convictions. Sound like anyone you know?"

Slowly she shook her head. She couldn't think of a single person she had met since she'd arrived in D.C. who had struck her as being that devout.

"Then maybe that's why they needed your brother."

Chapter Thirteen

In spite of the fact that it was broad daylight and John was right behind her, Kelly had to steel herself to open the front door of Chad's house. As soon as she did, the memory of what had happened last night became a nearly physical barrier to her entry.

She felt an indescribable sense of relief when she touched the switch inside the front door and light flooded the foyer. That simple act went a long way toward restoring her confidence, enough to allow her to step across the threshold. Although she knew that whoever had been hiding in the shower certainly wasn't here now, residual terror made her knees weak.

"The new codes are functional," John said.

She turned to find him studying the security system's response to the combination of numbers he'd just punched in. New locks. New codes. So why didn't she feel safe?

"Good," she said, pushing the word past the constriction in her throat.

"I want to take a look around."

Unwilling to let him out of her sight, she followed as he stepped past her. Whoever that bastard in the ski mask had been, she owed this unfamiliar sense of vulnerability to him.

John made straight for the hall bath, as she'd known he would. The police had searched it by flashlight last night. Given the limitations under which they'd been working, it wasn't really too surprising they'd found no trace of the man. But he damn well *had* been there, she reaffirmed to herself as she watched John examine the interior of the shower.

She stood in the doorway, unable to bring herself to walk into the room. After a moment or two, her eyes lifted to the mirrored ceiling.

It now reflected the man stooping down outside the shower stall, again balanced on the balls of his feet. His posture evoked both the dim safety of his office last night and the memory of his solicitude. The same concern that had caused him to keep watch outside her house last night.

He always seemed to be there when she needed him. The thought caused a tightness in her throat, the kind that usually accompanied tears. She fought them, recognizing the same emotion that had driven her into his arms the night they'd met.

"I knew there would be something," he said, drawing her gaze down from his reflection. He was on his hands and knees now, his head slanted to the side, almost parallel to the floor, as he peered across the black marble floor of the stall.

"What is it?"

"Footprints," he said, turning to meet her eyes.

Last night the cops had been adamant that there were no tracks leading into the house—despite the rain and mud it would create. And now…

"How can there be prints in there and not out here?" she asked, studying the shining expanse between them.

"Bend down and look *across* the surface," he suggested. He pushed up to his knees as he gave the directions.

Feeling foolish, she obeyed. Using the reflection of the overhead lights angled against the stone, she discovered what he'd seen. Although not tracks in the conventional sense, there *were* traffic patterns visible across the glossy surface.

"You have a repairman in here since this shower was last used?"

She glanced up to find his attention once more on the floor of the stall. "There haven't been *any* repairmen in here. Not since I've lived in the house."

"And you wouldn't be in the habit of wearing shoes when you shower, would you?" Amusement colored the question.

She felt a swell of vindication at the thought of what that must mean. "Is that what you're seeing? The print of a shoe?"

"Nothing that clear, but the impressions appear to be patterned. They're worth preserving."

"How do we do that?"

"If we can get the lens at the exact angle to the light, we can take a photograph of them. It might not be enough to use in court—"

"But it's enough to prove someone *was* here."

He straightened to look back at her, seeming surprised by her tone. "I never doubted that."

The police had. And they hadn't been overly careful about letting her know it.

"Do we take it to the cops? The picture, I mean."

"They won't do anything with it. They'd have to have something to match the prints to in order to make a case. Your brother have a camera?"

"Digital. Top of the line," she said.

Like everything else Chad had ever bought. In this case, she could only be grateful for that tendency.

SHE HAD ALREADY LOCATED the camera and was on her way back to give it to John when the phone rang. Her first inclination was to let the answering machine get it, but since she was in the bedroom, she crossed to the bedside table and picked it up on the third ring.

"Hello."

"Where the hell have you been?"

Mark Daniels's question seemed filled with equal parts of anger and anxiety. More of that big-brother complex he was suffering from.

"And how are you, Mark? It's nice to hear from you, too."

"I've been trying to get in touch with you all night, Kelly. Forgive me for being worried sick."

His sarcasm almost matched hers, but that didn't ease her guilt over leaving him to stew. She should have known he'd call.

"I'm sorry," she said, working to modify her tone. "The power went out. I didn't want to stay here in the dark."

It was obvious when the silence on the line expanded that her explanation had caught him off guard.

"You could have called," he said, sounding less angry. "I would have come to get you. You could have spent the night here."

"I managed," she said noncommittally.

Her eyes lifted to find John standing in the doorway. His brows rose in inquiry.

Putting her hand over the receiver, she mouthed the word "Mark." He nodded his understanding, but he didn't leave.

"Everything all right there now?" Daniels asked.

"It seems to be." Her answer again provided as little information as she thought she could get by with.

"You were going to call me about getting together."

She had forgotten he wanted to see her. His request of Sunday morning seemed like a distant memory.

"Sorry," she said, trying to sound contrite. "I've had a lot to do."

"How'd the board meeting go?"

"Okay, I suppose. The auction was a success in any case."

"They fight you on the money? About where it's going."

"They didn't have the opportunity. I haven't made a final decision about that yet."

"Don't let them browbeat you. Chad left you in charge. If you'd like for me to come with you to the next meeting—"

"I appreciate the thought, but as you say, Chad *did* leave me in charge."

"I only want to help, sweetheart. As Chad's friend, I—"

"I know," she interrupted again. "Listen, Mark, could I call you back later. I'm expecting someone."

There was no response for maybe four or five seconds.

"Not Edmonds, I hope."

"No, but it's interesting you would say that." Her eyes considered the man he'd mentioned, who was leaning against the doorjamb, arms crossed as he rather obviously waited for her to finish the call.

"He isn't what he seems."

"Really." She pronounced the word without any questioning inflection.

"*Don't* get involved with him."

"I'd be interested in knowing why you'd say that."

"I did some digging after I left your place yesterday. For one thing, he's a private investigator. The information made me reconsider the attack in the parking deck. That could easily have been staged to arrange an introduction."

That conclusion would be obvious once you knew John was an investigator. He had admitted he'd been following her.

"Why would he want that?"

"I'm working on finding out if it was just because he wanted to meet you. Or if he had some ulterior motive. In the meantime, stay away from him."

"I appreciate your concern," she said.

She didn't intend to take orders from Mark Daniels, but there was no need to fight that battle this morning. Something of her resentment must have come through in her reply, however.

"Don't get on your high horse, Kelly. I'm only doing what Chad would want me to."

"Chad never got over the notion that he was responsible for me. I suppose that was natural, given our situation, but you aren't my brother, Mark."

"That's the *last* thing I want to be, believe me."

"Then maybe you should think about backing off."

Another silence.

"Frankly I'm finding that difficult right now. I'm worried about your involvement with a man you know nothing about."

"That's exactly what I'm talking about."

"I had hoped that the two of us... Surely you must have some idea of how I feel about you. I was trying to give you time to come to terms with Chad's death before I broached the subject. Then I walk in there Sunday morning and find you've spent the night with a stranger."

She had known that Mark's interest wasn't completely platonic, but she had been hoping to avoid just such a scene as was playing out now. And with a very interested audience, she acknowledged, glancing up again to meet John's eyes. They seemed amused, although thankfully he could hear only one side of the conversation.

"That's none of your business," she said to Mark.

"I had hoped to *make* it my business."

"I don't mean to be rude, but I'm afraid that's out of the question."

"He's there, isn't he?"

Her delay gave her away.

"He's listening to every word you're saying," Mark concluded bitterly. "I hope to hell he's enjoying himself."

"If he is, he's the only one."

Another pause.

"Look," Mark said, modulating his voice so that the anger was no longer evident, "I care about you. If you aren't willing to accept my concern in any other way, accept it as the sister of my best friend. Whom I miss very much, by the way."

"I know you do," she said, touched despite everything by the raw emotion in his voice.

"And I want you to remember that you are a very wealthy woman. At the very least, we know Edmonds is an opportunist. I don't believe there was anything coincidental about your meeting."

There hadn't been. It had been far less coincidental than even Mark could imagine. Yet knowing that, and knowing also that John wouldn't hesitate to report anything detrimental he discovered about Chad, she had agreed to allow him to protect her. Maybe Mark was right. Maybe she did need a keeper.

"I'll remember," she said. "And now I really have to go, Mark."

"When can we get together? I want to do some more checking around about that guy—"

"Please don't. It's really not your concern."

"Call me."

Instead of making the promise he'd demanded, she pressed the off button with her thumb. As she did, she met John's eyes.

"Mark. I forgot to call him."

He nodded but didn't comment. Instead he held out his hand for the camera.

She walked toward him, intending to lay it on his outstretched palm. His eyes held hers, even when she stopped in front of him.

"He knew I was here," he said.

"He guessed."

"Obviously he didn't like the idea."

"Somehow he found out that you're a private investigator. He thinks the incident in the parking deck was staged to arrange a meeting with me."

"There's no way he could have found out what I do."

She hadn't even thought to wonder where Mark had acquired that information. Like Catherine, he had a lot of acquaintances in this town and the resources to hire the best information gatherers.

"I'm only telling you what he said."

"What did he say about the board?"

"Not to let them browbeat me."

"About the change in distribution? Did he know about that?"

She had mentioned the controversy to Mark. He knew most of the people involved, and he had always been willing to listen and give advice. Not that she could remember anything specific he'd advised her to do in this case. Nothing beyond that he'd told her about John today.

"He knew the board wasn't happy with what Chad had done last year."

"They'd discussed it? He and your brother?"

"I suppose. I mentioned that they were upset over the shift, and he didn't seem surprised. He didn't seem very interested, either. Other than to tell me that I shouldn't let them walk all over me. That was the kind of thing Chad would have said. That I should take charge. Speak up for myself. Maybe it was more of him trying to emulate Chad."

"It sounded just now as if he's tiring of playing big brother."

He had probably heard enough of the conversation to read between its lines the unwanted confession Mark had made.

"Or did you know that before today?" he asked.

"He hadn't said anything, but...I knew. I guess I was hoping he *wouldn't* say it."

John nodded, still holding her eyes. Then he released them, reaching for the camera. He took it and walked back down the hall to take the photograph of the prints in the shower.

While John was occupied with preserving the evidence from the black marble flooring, she decided to make her own survey of the house. She would be better qualified than the police to judge if anything had been disturbed. Besides, she had the advantage of light, enough to detect any sign of an intruder in the house.

She started in the back because that's where she believed the noise she'd heard had originated. It was unlikely that it had come from the area of the bedrooms, since she had been in Chad's when the man in the ski mask had entered the hall bath. Besides, it had sounded more distant.

She searched the pool and deck area, looking for something that might have been blown over by the wind. And there was nothing. None of the panes in the windows on the back had been tampered with. Of course, if John were right about the codes, then whoever had entered the house hadn't had to break in.

The formal living room and the dining room were next, but neither showed any evidence of intruders. Astonishingly, she couldn't remember having been in either of them before. Not in all the weeks she'd lived here.

The breakfast room and kitchen looked cheery in the morning light, unlike the shadowed obstacle course they'd been last night. The metal trashcan was slightly out of alignment with the base cabinet, but she had done that on her way to the garage. Since it had been dark at the time, she couldn't tell if it had been moved after she'd run into it.

"Anything?"

She turned to find John watching her.

"No," she admitted in frustration. "No broken glass. No forced entry. But I heard something break. I know I did."

"Maybe he was already here when you arrived. Maybe he broke something to lure you out of the tub."

The idea that he had been inside the house waiting for her was chilling, evoking the same horror she'd felt last night. Despite the light shining in through the sunporch, she shivered.

"If that's what he did—"

Without finishing the sentence, she walked over to the trashcan and lifted the lid. It was almost empty because she hadn't been home for meals in several days. In the bottom, resting on top of an outdated newspaper was a wad of paper towels.

She reached down into the can, but before her fingers could bring them out, John's hand fastened around her wrist. He was standing behind her, looking over her shoulder as he held her arm.

"Tongs," he ordered.

She knew there wouldn't be fingerprints on the paper, at least not recoverable ones, but it was possible that if what he'd said were true, there could be prints on whatever the intruder had wrapped up in the towels.

She straightened, suddenly very conscious of John's nearness. She tried to turn to obey his directive, but he didn't step back as she'd anticipated.

Her breast brushed against his chest. The contact was brief, but it was enough to provoke reaction. Her nipples tightened, in memory or anticipation.

There was an answering constriction within her lower body. Something hot and sweet and too fleeting.

Only then did he move, stepping back quickly enough that she couldn't legitimately protest his proximity. Without comment, she walked over to the drawers where the utensils were kept, pulling them open one by one until she found a pair of salad tongs. As she handed them to him, their eyes met.

That contact was equally brief. He broke it, bending to use the tongs to bring up the wad of paper. As he laid it on the granite counter, there was an unmistakable clink of glass.

She moved closer as he began to peel the towels back to reveal what they'd heard. Inside was one of the heavy tumblers Chad favored. If she opened the cabinet doors above their heads, they would be lined up in precise rows, except for the one that now lay shattered, enclosed in the paper towels.

"He probably broke it on the countertop," John offered.

The stone surface would be hard enough to accomplish that without leaving any marks. The quality of the paper towels would have prevented the glass from scattering all over the room, yet they would be light enough not to muffle the noise. After all, as John had said, that had obviously been the purpose of this whole exercise. To lure her out here.

"I don't understand. Why would he want me in the kitchen?"

He didn't answer for several seconds. Then he raised his eyes from the broken glass to meet hers.

"Maybe he thought there were more possibilities."

"Possibilities for what?"

Again he hesitated, and when he finally answered her question, she understood why.

"For something different enough from what happened to Chad that no one would think to question it."

"Like what?"

Even as she asked, she was beginning to come to grips with what he was suggesting. The intruder had wanted to lure her to the back of the house to kill her, but in a way that couldn't be tied to her brother's untimely death.

"Suicide, maybe," John said.

The word created a coldness in the bottom of her stomach. Despite her immediate instinct to deny the ridiculousness of that idea, she knew a lot of people might buy into it.

They'd say she was despondent over her brother's death. Suffering from a sense of letdown and grief, having completed his final project. Dreading the responsibility of carrying on his work, a feeling she'd made no secret of. Removed from both her friends and her life.

It was a believable scenario. As the attack in the parking deck might have been. She couldn't think of a single person in her life who would question either of them too closely.

"Was I supposed to stick my head in the oven?"

She had been trying for flippancy, but it hadn't quite come off. Instead, her voice reflected both the anger she felt and the anguish of her isolation. An isolation that had just been brought home to her with chilling force.

In spite of his ultimatum last night, John put his arm around her, pulling her against the solid strength of his body. She didn't even think about resisting. Just as when she'd slept in his arms, she felt safe here. Protected. And because of that it was easier to ask the next question.

"Okay, not the oven. Then why here?"

"Proximity to the garage, maybe."

"He was going to put me in the car and start the engine?"

"It's a possibility."

She could tell from his voice that he didn't want to talk about this. Neither did she, of course, but she needed to know what she was up against. And the idea he'd just broached had never crossed her mind.

"If this was supposed to be a suicide, how did he think he would get me into the car without a struggle?"

"We should probably have the glass on the rim of the tub analyzed."

She pushed far enough away to look up at him. "It's bourbon," she said. "I poured it myself. *After* I got home."

"You were out of the bathroom long enough for him to have doctored it. All he had to do was to wait for you to come back and finish it off."

"I came into the house this way. If he wanted to attack me, why didn't he do it then?"

"I don't know. Maybe he wasn't here then. Or maybe the plan was to wait for you to go to sleep. Maybe he got rattled by something and decided to improvise."

"Because he saw you parked outside?" she speculated.

He thought about it. "If he knew my car."

"It was in the driveway all Saturday night."

''Then let's assume he recognized it. Maybe he was afraid I'd get tired of waiting out in the rain...''

''And come inside,'' she said. It was a reasonable assumption. He'd already spent one night in this house. ''And that meant he had to change whatever he'd been planning.''

''Either that or give it up entirely. And if he was already in the house...'' John shrugged.

''Whoever he is,'' she said bitterly, ''he seems to be in a hurry to get this done.''

His arm tightened around her comfortingly. ''Running scared. You remember that. *He's* the one who's running scared.''

Chapter Fourteen

"Are you sure you want to do this?" John asked, as he held the door of the SUV for her.

"No, but I don't think we have a choice."

Not after the picture he'd painted of what he believed the intruder had intended last night. Someone wanted her dead. Enough that they'd already made two attempts.

She could no longer doubt his assessment of her risk. Just as she didn't doubt the timeline under which they were working.

"We could start with someone else."

They could, of course, but approaching Catherine Suttle first had its advantages, all of which they'd already discussed. The older woman was closely attuned to the other members of the board. She probably knew what they were saying behind Kelly's back. Maybe, even more important, what they were feeling and *not* saying.

She was also a potential source of information about the shadowy organization Chad had begun to support with Legacy money last year. A support that might have cost him his life.

"If anybody can put the pieces of the puzzle together for us," she said, "it's Catherine."

"And you trust her enough to lay this out for her? After all, there's no guarantee she isn't part of it."

"You haven't met her," Kelly said confidently.

She got out of the car, looking at the mansion in front of her. Impeccably landscaped and lovingly maintained, the Georgian-style house was a fitting setting for the woman they had come to see. A woman who couldn't possibly be involved in something as sordid as murder. Especially not the murder of friends.

"*They* don't wear signs, either," John said, taking her elbow as they made their way up the walk.

He told her that about terrorists. Now he was reminding her that murderers didn't give themselves away by their actions, either.

It would be far easier if they did. None of the people she'd met in Washington, neither the board members or Chad's friends and acquaintances who had offered their support during these difficult weeks, seemed to be the kind who would deal in death and destruction.

Not on a mass scale. Not even on a personal one. That seemed totally removed from the world they occupied.

Now she knew it wasn't. Her brother was dead, and two attempts had been made on her own life. If it hadn't been for the man walking by her side…

"We can play it by ear," she conceded.

This dark world of death and destruction was John's environment. One he was infinitely familiar with. Both his judgment and his instincts had been far more attuned to what was happening within it than hers had been.

For her, being the target of a murderer had presented another steep learning curve. One she had to master quickly or it would be too late.

"I SEE THAT CLAIRE'S been holding out on me," Catherine said as she ushered them into a sunlit sitting room.

"Claire?" Kelly questioned.

"Claire Cabot. I'm assuming this one belongs to her Griff." When neither of them responded, Catherine's smile widened. "You can tell me, but then you'd have to kill me. Is that how it goes?"

"I don't work for Cabot," John said.

There was no need to get into the reasons for that. And there was always the chance the old woman would let it go.

"But you know who he is. I thought you might. All of you have that same look about you."

He didn't ask what kind of look she made reference to. He knew.

"Or maybe," he suggested, "I *also* have good sources."

"Of course. *That's* why you're here. I confess I've been wondering. You're interested in my connections."

"I told John that you know everyone in Washington," Kelly put in.

"I'm flattered, but I'm afraid I've already told you all I know about Griff's organization. Private, discreet and very good. I hear they are also very expensive if you can afford them and pro bono if you can't. Shouldn't be a problem for you, my dear," she added, focusing faded blue eyes, fringed by impossibly long, darkened lashes, on Kelly.

"It isn't the Phoenix we've come to see you about," she said.

Penciled brows arched in surprise. Instead of asking for more information, Catherine issued an invitation.

"Why don't we have some tea before we play 'Who Do You Know?' Or would you prefer something stronger? We don't observe drinking hours here. All that ridiculous sun-over-the-yardarm stuff. I've always felt that if you needed a Scotch, no matter what time of day it is, you should have it.''

''Nothing for me, thank you,'' Kelly said.

''And you?'' Catherine asked John, her manner almost arch.

''I'm fine,'' he said.

''Yes, indeed you are.''

There was an amused gleam in her eyes. She was obviously enjoying his discomfiture with her flirting.

Thankfully, she didn't prolong the moment. She gestured toward the cream-colored sofa, indicating that they should sit there. She took the chair opposite the couch, perching on the edge of its seat.

Her back was as straight as if she were still a student in Mrs. Porter's School for Young Ladies. Her knees, held tightly together, slanted to one side of the chair, ankles gracefully crossed on the other to showcase legs that were still slim and shapely.

''Then, civilities aside, what can I do for you?'' she asked as soon as they were seated.

''Tell us what you know about The Covenant,'' he said.

Catherine's eyes widened slightly. Her gaze focused on Kelly's face for a few seconds before it returned to his.

''I know that membership is highly secret. That the organization is dedicated to propagating Judeo-Christian ethics within government,'' she said, ticking off the points as if she were reading them from a list. ''That mission is stated nowhere in print, by the way. At least nowhere I'm aware of.''

''Why?'' he interrupted.

''None of their goals are. If you're approached to join, it's done privately. Usually by a trusted friend. There's no literature. No membership drives. No advertisements.''

''Have *you* been approached?'' Kelly asked.

"If I had been, I couldn't tell you. Not if I'd accepted."

"And if you hadn't accepted?" John asked.

"Then I could tell you that none of my trusted friends would be so foolish," she said with a smile.

He was aware that she hadn't answered his question. Nor was she likely to. It was becoming more evident as the conversation progressed that Catherine Suttle would tell them as much as she wanted to and no more.

If he weren't persona non grata at the Phoenix, he could have asked Griff for this information. Or even Claire Cabot's grandfather, who had been a member of the Washington scene at least as long as Ms. Suttle. Neither would have ever been in danger of being tempted to join some pseudo-sacred secret society.

"What else do you know, Catherine?" Kelly urged, bringing the old woman's attention back to her.

"I can tell you that the group claims to be the descendent of an ancient and even more secret organization, one to which many of this country's founding fathers purportedly belonged. I've always wondered if the story were apocryphal. A need for reflected glory or a desire for legitimacy. Whatever the case, the modern incarnation is at least a century old."

"Do you know any of the current leaders?" Kelly asked.

"If I told you that, then *I'd* have to kill *you*," Catherine said, smiling at her.

Given what had happened the past few days, John didn't find the witticism remotely amusing. "So you *do* know them?"

As he posed the question, John wondered if this interview could possibly result in any worthwhile information. The old woman obviously relished her role as both a repository of secrets and a true Beltway insider. As yet she had told them nothing that wasn't common knowledge.

"A few. Why don't you tell me first why you're so interested in The Covenant?"

Kelly's eyes found his, seeking permission. He didn't give it. The decision of how much they could trust Catherine Suttle would have to be hers.

His instincts were that the woman was not going to give them anything of value until she'd gotten something in exchange. As with most people who valued being considered an insider, information was her most coveted medium of trade. Whether that made her dangerous or simply inquisitive he couldn't tell.

"You know that I've been concerned about the changes that were made this past year in the distribution of the Legacy," Kelly said, choosing her words with care.

"They might be secret, but The Covenant has long been a recognized force for good in this town. Are you questioning your brother's decision to add them to the foundation?"

"I'm trying to understand how he came to that decision."

"Obviously because he thought it was the right thing to do."

"And you agree with that?" John asked.

"I agree that he *thought* that. Would I have given that much money to them if it were up to me? The answer is no. That doesn't mean, however, that Chad shouldn't have."

"But…why would he?" Kelly probed. "It seems so unlike something Chad would be interested in."

"Why? I imagine for the same reasons most of us choose a cause. Or a religion. Or even a football team. There's something that draws us at that time in our lives in that particular direction."

"And you weren't angry when his largess to The Covenant took money away from your own projects?'' John asked.

"Why should I be angry? It wasn't my money. People gave it with the understanding that Chad would spend it for a worthy cause. Even if it weren't my cause, the way the Legacy was set up from the beginning, he had every right to use the funds we raised for whatever he wanted. I don't understand why you're questioning that.''

"Because I think someone murdered him,'' Kelly said. Her voice was low, but firm.

Seconds ticked off as John waited for Catherine's response. Despite the widening of her eyes when they had first mentioned The Covenant, there was virtually no reaction to the suggestion that Chad Lockett had been murdered. And he found that more than curious.

"That's ridiculous,'' she said finally.

"Chad wasn't careless,'' Kelly said. "Or reckless. Not with his own life. And that plane had just undergone a full maintenance inspection.''

"Accidents happen,'' Catherine said almost dismissively. "I know his death at such a young age was difficult for you to accept. Believe me, no one understands more than I do how hard it is to lose someone who was so alive—''

"And there have been subsequent attacks on me,'' Kelly went on, as if Catherine had not spoken.

"Attacks?''

Catherine's shock was a noticeable contrast to her previous calmness. The problem was John couldn't tell how genuine it was.

"The first in the parking deck after the auction. That's when I met John. He came to my rescue.''

The faded blue eyes focused briefly on his face. In

the fraction of a second he had to study them, they seemed cold.

Almost immediately, Catherine turned back to Kelly to demand, "Where the hell was security? We pay enough to those bastards."

"They'd been told they were free to leave at midnight," John said.

The carmined lips tightened, revealing a pattern of tiny lines around their carefully drawn outline. "Fools."

"That wasn't your decision, I take it?"

"If there's one thing I've never been, young man, it's a fool. Probably some more of Hugh's cost-cutting crap. It won't happen again, I can promise you that. If we can't provide our guests with the assurance that they can come and go without being molested—" She stopped abruptly. "Good Lord, girl, you don't believe someone at the foundation deliberately released security in order to facilitate an attack on you? That's as ridiculous as the idea that Chad was murdered."

"There was an intruder in the house last night," Kelly said, her voice remarkably restrained considering the episode she was recounting. "He wore a ski mask over his face, and he was hiding in the shower. Taken together…" She allowed the sentence to trail without stating the obvious.

There was a long silence. The old woman's eyes pinned hers as if she were trying to decide if Kelly were serious.

"I can find out," she said finally.

"Who was in the house?"

Her eyes flicked back to John at his question. "Of course not." Her tone assigned him to the same category of fool who would let security go before the last of the guests had left the party. "Even *my* sources aren't that good. I meant

The Covenant. You want to know who the main players are. Give me a couple of days. I'll call you.''

"No, Catherine. I can't allow you to ask questions that might put you in jeopardy," Kelly said.

"You can't stop me. Beside, those bastards aren't going to mess with me."

"The Covenant?" John asked, willing to be considered a fool to obtain more information. "Or someone on the board?"

"I meant The Covenant, but I'm not afraid of either."

"Maybe you should be," he warned.

"First of all, I don't think there was anything suspicious about Chad's death. That's Kelly's grief talking. And believe me, I understand grief. Secondly, just because someone screwed up the security arrangements, that doesn't mean there's some nefarious plot afoot against her, either. Why would there be?"

"Because someone's afraid she'll change the funding structure of the Legacy," he suggested.

"If that were the case, then why would they want Chad dead? You can't have it both ways. Either they want the distribution to remain the same or they want it to be done differently. You've made no secret of your concern about the changes Chad instituted," she added, turning to Kelly. "If you believe someone killed him because they didn't like the way the money was being distributed, then why would they attack you when you've given every indication that you plan to change it back?"

"*You* thought that's what Kelly intended to do?" John asked.

"Plain as the nose on your face. Especially Sunday. All those questions about why we thought Chad had made that decision. I knew you wouldn't leave it that way. Not after some of the others got to you."

"The first attack was *before* the board meeting," Kelly said.

"In an unsecured parking deck? On the night of a well-publicized charity auction? And in that section of town? Speaking of which, we really have to think about a change in location for the future. Put that on the agenda for the next meeting, why don't you? In the meantime, I'll ream someone out about the security snafu. I've a pretty good idea where to start with that."

"Please don't," Kelly said. "We can handle that at the meeting, too. I'm sure you're right about it having nothing to do with last night's attack. It was probably just an oversight on someone's part. I'll handle it, I promise."

John knew Kelly didn't believe that. She was trying to keep Catherine out of trouble—or keep her from making trouble.

Of course, it would be natural for Kelly to come to her with the security problem, since Catherine had been chairman of the event. Anyone she approached would probably credit her concern to that.

"It would be better not to bring that up at all until we know more about what's going on," he warned.

Catherine turned toward him, her expression considering. "You may be right," she said. "I'll leave it up to you, as long as you keep me informed about the course of your investigation.

"And there's no need to look at me like that," she went on when he didn't respond to that demand. "I told you I'm not a fool. She isn't hanging around with you for your good looks, as tempting as those might be. You're in this up to your neck, and although I'm a bit doubtful of the coincidence of your parking deck rescue, I have to say I'm relieved. I tend to go with my instinct about people. They aren't always right, but in this case, I'm banking on you being one of the good guys. I'm warning you, though. Don't prove me wrong. I have a long memory for people who hurt my friends.''

''So do I,'' he said, his eyes conveying his own warning.

The challenge provoked a burst of what seemed to be truly delighted laughter. Catherine threw back her head and brayed in a manner that could in no way be called ladylike. When her amusement subsided, she didn't seem in the least embarrassed by her outburst.

''You can keep this one,'' she advised Kelly, her smile still wide. ''I like a man who retains that slightly uncivilized 'Mess with what's mine at your peril' attitude. I'm not the only woman who finds it attractive, especially in this town full of apologist sissies. As long as he can back it up, that is. Can you?'' she asked bluntly, turning her attention to him once more.

''I intend to try,'' he promised. It was a vow that was as much for Kelly's benefit as for Catherine Suttle's.

Chapter Fifteen

"My place or yours?" he asked.

Kelly had been staring through the windshield since they'd left Catherine Suttle's. He was aware that she turned toward him at his question, but he kept his eyes on the road.

"Yours, please. If that's all right."

"Probably the smart thing to do," he said casually, despite the small lurch in the bottom of his stomach. "Our involvement won't be secret much longer, but for right now, my apartment is less well known to whoever this is than your brother's house."

Our involvement. He was involved with her now on so many levels it was increasingly difficult to separate the purely personal from the professional.

Despite the fact that he'd been fired, he still wanted to know why a reference to the Legacy had been in those terrorist-linked transmissions Ethan Snow had run across. Even if it turned out to have nothing to do with the attempts on Kelly's life.

A desire driven by patriotism? Or by the need to prove that Griff's judgment of him had been faulty? In any case, neither was as important as the need to protect Kelly. And that was definitely personal.

"She was wrong, you know," Kelly said.

This time he did glance at her, but she was still facing the front. "Wrong about what?"

"I *hadn't* made up my mind about the distribution. If anything, I was leaning toward keeping it as it was. I thought that's what Chad intended to do. And I was determined that if they'd killed him in hopes of forcing a different allocation of the money, then I'd be damned if they were going to get what they wanted."

"Catherine sounded convinced."

"I know. That's what bothers me. I'm wondering if she really made that judgment at the board table. Or if she had some help in coming to that conclusion."

"What kind of help?"

"Maybe someone suggested to her that I was going to make a change. Then, when she heard whatever I said at the table, she took it to mean something it didn't."

"How could you possibly determine that without asking her?"

"I couldn't, I suppose. Not definitively. But I'd be interested in hearing someone else's take."

"A second opinion about how your comments came across?"

"To see if I really did come on that strongly about changing things. If so, then I'll have to give Catherine the benefit of the doubt."

"And if not?"

"Then I'll have wonder who influenced her to believe something that wasn't true."

"NOT TO ME, you didn't," Bertha Reynolds said in answer to Kelly's carefully phrased question about whether she'd sounded as if her mind were made up. "I knew you were upset over the infighting. I had been feeling as if I should tell you that's just how we do things. We talk too much and too loudly. I thought you should know that it didn't mean a thing.

"But, for what it's worth, I didn't think you'd made up your mind. If anything, I had the impression that you intended to go along with the decisions Chad had made. To honor his memory. His last wish, so to speak, for the Legacy."

"Then you didn't interpret my questions as dissatisfaction with the distribution?"

"It seemed to me that you didn't really care which organization got what. You just wanted to understand why Chad had made the change."

"And you don't have a clue about that, Bertha? It could be important."

"I don't think Leon was far off the mark. Somebody talked Chad into it. Given how he felt about the Legacy, it would have had to be someone whose opinion he trusted implicitly."

"What do you know about The Covenant, Ms. Reynolds?" John interjected.

"I've heard they do good works, but that's not my cup of tea, I'm afraid."

Damned with faint praise, Kelly thought.

"Do you know anyone who's a member?"

Dark eyes, magnified by those thick lenses, focused on John's. "Anyone on the board, do you mean?"

"*Is* there someone?"

"Not that I'm aware of. I always wondered how Chad came to add them to the mix. An organization that's so different from the rest."

"But you didn't have a problem with part of the money going to them. As it was in the beginning, I mean."

"Not at all. And not as it was at the end, either. It was

Chad's prerogative to decide. The only problem for me was the lack of notification to the other charities that such a major shift in funding was coming. It seemed unprofessional, almost unkind, to do that to them without any warning.''

And her brother was neither, Kelly thought. It was almost as if whoever had made that decision had been someone other than Chad.

"Now what?" John asked, as they pulled out of the parking lot of the apartment complex where Bertha lived. The contrast between its genteel poverty and the opulence of the Suttle house had been marked. As had that between Catherine's confident assertions and Bertha's near diffidence.

And the two had had equally differing views about Kelly's state of mind during the meeting. He wasn't sure, even if she wanted to pursue it, that he should sanction her getting a third opinion. He hoped that wasn't what she was about to suggest.

"Home, I guess."

The slip seemed unthinking, and he tried to ignore its implications. It was too much to believe that in the one night she'd spent there, she had come to consider his apartment ''home'' in any sense of the word. Since they'd discussed the decision earlier, however, he turned in the direction of his place rather than her brother's without seeking further clarification.

"I can't think of anyone who might have that type of influence over Chad," Kelly said, obviously still thinking about what Bertha had told them.

"You," he suggested.

"If I'd wanted it. I didn't. At the beginning of all this,

I told him to do what he thought was right. He never consulted me on those decisions because he understood that.''

"Girlfriend, maybe?''

"None of his relationships had that kind of clout. Not that I'm aware of.''

"Would you have been?''

"Maybe not. Not unless he was serious about her.''

"And you didn't get that kind of impression about any of them in say...the last year or so?''

"I haven't gotten that kind of impression in more than five years. And that particular relationship lasted maybe six months. I *did* get to meet her, which was rare.''

"He didn't bring them home to the family?''

She laughed. "Rarely. My brother enjoyed being a bachelor. He'd made it his primary pastime. Along with the Legacy.''

"How about Daniels's influence? You said they were best friends.''

"They went to school together. Roomed together a couple of years. Crewed and played polo. I'm not sure any of those things would have made Chad trust him to decide on issues involving the Legacy. If he did consult Mark, neither of them mentioned it to me.''

"Other close friends?''

"Close? That's relative, I guess. Chad had hundreds of friends, and he shamelessly took advantage of each of them for his projects. Everyone on the board could be considered a friend. Most of the people at the auction.''

"Then we'll think of another approach,'' he soothed, sensing her growing frustration with an investigation that seemed to be going nowhere.

They didn't even know for sure if they were on the right track in thinking that the change in allocation was at the heart of whatever was going on. And it was quite a leap from The Covenant, a society interested in infusing Judeo-Christian ethics into national politics, to an involvement in terrorism.

He couldn't think of anything other than the Legacy's millions of dollars, however, that would make someone target both Kelly and her brother. Of course, there was always the possibility that she was wrong about Chad's accident.

"Maybe I should ask him," Kelly said.

Him? "Daniels?"

"He's been saying he needs to talk to me. And he knows I've got to make a decision on the distribution within the next few days. I didn't put the two together, but…it's possible, I suppose. And even if that isn't what he wants to talk about, I could ask him if he heard Chad say anything about who or what got him interested in The Covenant. Mark's known him longer than any of the others."

"You want to do that now? Before we head back to the apartment?"

He didn't relish that encounter. Despite her seeming disinterest, Daniels was an attractive man who was obviously infatuated with Kelly. He was also someone who now viewed John as a rival. For that reason alone, it wouldn't be a comfortable interview.

"I doubt that's what Mark had in mind when he said we needed to talk. A conversation involving the three of us."

"If he wants to talk to you right now, that's what he's going to get."

"He isn't going to like it."

"I don't give a damn what he likes. Somebody's trying to kill you. Until we find out who, there aren't going to be any private conversations. Not with anyone."

"You could stand at the door with your gun drawn."

There was something about her voice that made him turn

to look at her. Even in profile, the tilt at the corner of her lips was evident. And he was infinitely relieved to see it.

She was surrounded by people she had once trusted and could trust no longer. Someone had made two attempts on her life, and she believed that whoever that was had murdered her brother. Deep inside, however, as evidenced by that teasing smile, there were untapped reserves of strength and courage. He was afraid she was going to need them before this was over.

"What makes you think I'm going to be willing to stand at the door? I was thinking about gun drawn and sitting in the chair opposite him," he said, his tone matching hers.

"I can't believe Mark's involved in this. He and Chad were like brothers. Besides…"

She paused, deliberately turning to look at him, but he kept his eyes on the road. He suspected the slight smile he'd glimpsed before was now more open.

"Besides, he says he's in love with you," he finished for her. "I know. That makes him all the more dangerous."

"Dangerous?" He wasn't sure if the amusement he heard in her repetition of the word was at Daniels's expense or his own.

"Love *and* money," he reminded her. "The oldest motives in the world for murder."

THEY HADN'T BEEN in the apartment more than five minutes when the doorbell rang. As he eased the Glock from the back holster where he'd been wearing it under his blazer all afternoon, John glanced toward the hallway.

If Kelly had heard the bell, she'd wisely decided not to put in an appearance. He could only trust that she'd continue to stay out of sight.

He crossed the room to put his eye against the peephole in the center of the door. The man standing in the hallway outside wasn't the last person he would have expected to show up here, but it would be close. Given the scenario surrounding his departure from the Phoenix, he realized he probably shouldn't be surprised to find that Ethan Snow was paying him a visit.

Using his left hand, John turned the dead bolt and then the knob and opened the door. His right still held his weapon, although once he'd identified his visitor, he had turned the muzzle so that it was pointing upward.

"Ethan," he said, stepping back to allow the Phoenix operative to enter.

"You under siege?" Snow asked. His questioning of the drawn weapon held a hint of amusement.

"You might say that," John answered, ignoring it. He closed the door behind his visitor and threw the bolt.

"Griff told me what happened," Ethan said as soon as it had been secured. "I figured there was more to the story than the bare-bones recital I got. When he's upset, he has a tendency to cut to the chase."

"To be fair, there wasn't much to tell. He thought I stepped over the line on the Lockett surveillance."

"And you feel you didn't."

"It was a very fine line." John smiled at the irony.

"They always are," Ethan acknowledged. "I've trampled a few myself. We all have at one time or another, even Griff, although he would probably deny it now. Whatever happened, I'm sorry he released you. You belong with the Phoenix. I told Griff that, for what it's worth."

Snow's vote of confidence might not have swayed Cabot, but the fact that he'd offered it eased some of the bitterness John had been harboring.

"Maybe if this had been the first time we'd disagreed…" He shrugged as if it didn't matter.

"I don't think I ever said thanks for what you did for

Elizabeth and Rafe. If it's any comfort, I hope that in your place I would have done the same."

"Yeah? Well, *you* might have gotten away with it."

There was a fractional lift of Snow's shoulders. "Those of us in the field have to react to the situation. Griff gets to make the hard calls."

"He didn't seem to mind making this one."

"He minded enough that he told me about it."

"Are you saying he *sent* you here?" Snow's hesitation in responding gave him his answer. "No, I didn't think so."

"I'll be taking over the Lockett matter, so I thought I should touch base with you," Ethan went on as if the question hadn't been asked. "See if you'd uncovered anything I should be aware of."

John had known Cabot wouldn't let this die. It was too important. And the head of the Phoenix had no way of knowing that he hadn't dropped the investigation. *Or* the surveillance.

"I don't have a problem with that. As long as it cuts both ways."

His visitor's slate-gray eyes narrowed. "You're still working it?"

"Just not for the Phoenix," Kelly said. She was standing at the entrance to the hallway, obviously listening to their conversation.

"Ms. Lockett," Ethan said, inclining his head. That hint of amusement was back in his deep voice.

"And you are?"

For the first time, John detected the haughtiness he'd expected the heir of the Lockett millions to exhibit before he'd met her.

"I'm Ethan Snow."

"You work for Cabot."

"Even before the Phoenix was formed," John explained. Ethan had been one of the original members of the black-ops CIA team Griff had created and trained.

"I told Cabot I wasn't interested in his services," Kelly said. "It seems we have an inherent conflict of interest."

"Ma'am?"

"You think my brother was dealing with terrorists. I don't."

"The name of the organization your brother founded turned up in transmissions between financial institutions known to be funneling money to extremist groups."

"And those financial institutions handle only terrorist money?"

There was a small movement at one corner of Ethan's mouth. "No, they don't."

"Then I would think that might explain why some mention of the Legacy was found there. I don't think we have anything else to talk about, Mr. Snow."

"How about the two attempts that have been made on your life?"

They had discussed the attack in the parking lot with Griff, but not what had happened last night; however, that information was available from the police department record, of course. Ethan had evidently done his homework.

"I believe those were carried out by the same people who killed my brother. Maybe Chad discovered the link you did. According to his computer's log, he spent a lot of time in the weeks before his death examining last year's financial records. Maybe that was his normal procedure when he was about to make a decision about the coming year's allocation, but it's also possible something was bothering him."

"You think something had made him suspicious."

"Maybe," she said. "It would explain the hours he'd spent on those statements."

"He didn't really know where the money was going," Ethan suggested, "and when he found out—"

"They killed him to prevent him from putting a stop to it. That makes more sense than Mr. Cabot's suggestion that my brother was willfully funding terrorism."

"Since you believe he wasn't, would you be willing to provide us with the complete financial records of his organization? *Your* organization," Ethan corrected.

"Why should I?"

"I would think you'd prefer our review of them to that of the government."

It was obviously a threat, and John knew it wasn't an idle one. Kelly wasn't a Phoenix client. Even if she had been, for Griff and the others, the nation's security would always take precedence. Love of country guaranteed they wouldn't let a concern for anyone's reputation, not even that of a client, keep them from doing what was right.

He felt the same way. He'd been up front with Kelly about that from the first. If he found anything to indicate her brother had been guilty of supplying money to terrorists, he would report it so the pipeline could be shut down.

"Someone cleaned out his computer," John said. "I can show you the distribution Lockett authorized and the information on their spending that the charities provided him with. I haven't had time to verify that what he *wanted* done with the Legacy money was, in fact, what *was* done."

"Do you have any objections to that, Ms. Lockett?"

"Would it do any good for me to object?"

"You could delay the inevitable," Ethan said, "but someone's going to look at those records. If it's the Phoenix, and we find nothing to connect your brother's organization, or the charities it supports, to extremist groups, that will go a long way toward clearing up any suspicion of him.''

''I can ask the accountant to supply you with the Legacy's financial statements. I'm not sure how much that will tell you about the use of the money once it's been distributed. That was all in Chad's records, some of which I saved in trying to understand them. He tried to vet the organizations he supported, but he couldn't guarantee what they would do with the money they were given. No one could.''

''It's always possible the collection was legitimate but the destination wasn't. We won't know that until we examine the records confirming exactly where the money went.''

''I'll call Hugh and see how soon I can get you that information,'' Kelly said, giving in to the inevitable.

Although she hadn't asked for his advice, John was relieved she'd made that decision. He'd feel more confident with the Phoenix, and their connections within the CIA, tracing the money trail than trying to do it on his own. It relieved some of the pressure and left him to do the job that he considered to be his primary responsibility—protecting Kelly Lockett from whoever had twice tried to kill her.

Chapter Sixteen

"You weren't surprised, were you?" Kelly asked.

She had made the phone call to Hugh Donaldson, while John had made sure the apartment was secure, checking windows and bolting the doors. Now she was watching him put supper together for the two of them in his small kitchen.

"That the Phoenix is pursuing this?" he questioned, looking up from the peppers he was chopping. "Not at that. I didn't expect whoever they put on it to contact me. Knowing Ethan, he probably did that on his own."

"You like him," she said, reading that in his voice.

"I respect him. I respect *all* of them. That's why I wanted to be a part of what they're doing."

"If it weren't for me, you would be."

It was a guilt she had nursed since Snow's comment about John belonging with the Phoenix. He did. Despite her earlier doubts, he had proven his integrity over and over again.

"How do you figure that's your fault?" His hands stilled as he turned to look at her.

"If we hadn't…gotten involved that night, you'd still be working for them."

"If we hadn't slept together."

She had deliberately avoided a more direct terminology.

She was still uncomfortable at the speed with which they'd ended up making love. It wasn't that she regretted trusting him. Not now. It was that it had complicated a relationship that, both for her safety and his job security, should have been strictly professional.

"That *is* what Cabot objected to, isn't it?"

"It was one thing he didn't like, but not the only one. He thought I should have intervened in what was happening in the parking deck and faded back out of sight. Then I should have turned the case over to another agent the next morning. As you know, I did neither."

"Why didn't you? If you knew your job might be on the line."

There was a beat of silence before he answered. "I imagine you can figure that out."

"*Because* we'd slept together."

"Give the lady a star," he said easily. He lifted the chopping board and, placing the edge of it over the waiting saucepan, scraped peppers, mushrooms and onions into it. "Not telling Griff was my decision. And my mistake. He called me on it. It had nothing to do with you."

"That's a stretch."

"The decision not to tell Griff about what happened that night had nothing to do with you," he repeated. "I thought he wouldn't find out. And I wanted to keep the case."

"So you don't kiss and tell. That shouldn't be a crime. Not even to the Phoenix."

"It is if it compromises the investigation."

"But it *didn't*. You aren't even working for Cabot anymore, and you're still playing by his rules."

"Honor among thieves," he said, smiling at her.

It was slightly twisted, but it was still a smile. Her heart ached for his loss. Until she'd seen him with Ethan Snow tonight, she hadn't understood how much belonging to the Phoenix had meant to him.

"Just honor," she said softly. "I'm told that's an old-fashioned concept."

"I'm an old-fashioned kind of guy."

"Just a sucker for a lady in distress."

He had told her that the night they met. The first time he'd come to her rescue.

He laughed. "Maybe so. Both times I've screwed myself up with Griff there was a woman involved."

A woman. *Another* woman. The idea of John involved with someone else, especially in the same kind of relationship they'd had, caused a reactive tightening of her stomach muscles. Considering the short time she'd known him, and that she had been the one to decide their relationship should remain strictly professional, her jealousy seemed out of proportion. As well as rather dog in the manger.

"Another lady in distress?" she asked, careful to keep any trace of either from her tone.

"The man she was in love with was in danger. Griff had promised him that the Phoenix would stay out of the situation, and that they would keep her safe, even if they had to hold her prisoner to do it. She wasn't interested in being safe. All she wanted was a chance to help him."

"You let her go," she guessed.

"*And* gave her my weapon and car." There was a trace of satisfaction in his recounting of what he'd done, despite what it had cost him.

"No wonder Cabot was angry," she said, smiling at the thought of the self-possessed head of the Phoenix being one-upped like that.

"Griff doesn't get angry. As they say, he just gets even."

The fragrance of the sautéing vegetables had begun to fill the kitchen. He added a splash of the wine he'd chosen to go with dinner and then poured a generous portion into each of the two goblets he'd set out on the counter. He picked his up, holding her eyes as he tasted the merlot. He raised his glass in a gesture of acceptance.

She picked hers up, but didn't drink from it immediately. She held it instead as she watched him stir the food. His hands were darkly tanned and so obviously powerful.

That they were now engaged in what was usually deemed a feminine task didn't detract in the least from his masculinity. She doubted anything could.

"So how did he get even with you?" she asked.

She didn't really care about his relationship with Cabot. She just wanted him to keep talking. She couldn't remember him addressing this many words to her since they'd discussed the menu at next year's auction. *After* he'd put himself at risk to ensure that if she wanted to be there for that one, she would be able to.

"By giving me meaningless assignments. Surveillance. He only trusted me to handle things that didn't matter."

"Like me?"

The question sounded bitter, but why should she resent Cabot's initial lack of interest in this case? After all, she hadn't wanted the Phoenix's interference. She had wanted to figure it all out for herself. To protect Chad's reputation and the reputation of the organization.

She should probably be relieved that the founder of the Phoenix hadn't considered what he believed her brother had done to be serious enough to rate a real agent. A least not at the beginning.

"*You* didn't fall into that category," John said. "I'd complained about the meaningless stuff, so Cabot got merciful and gave me a real case. Apparently he didn't expect me to really pursue it."

In no way could that be considered surveillance.

"You did, anyway."

"The attack in the parking deck didn't make sense. Taken along with what Ethan had found…" He shrugged, letting the explanation trail. This was ground they'd been over before.

"Maybe when you get to the bottom of whatever's going on, Cabot will reconsider."

"Even if he did, I couldn't take another year of surveillance."

Apparently if Cabot *were* willing to take him back, his pride wouldn't let him agree. Another wave of guilt washed over her.

"There might be a position available with the foundation."

As soon as the offer left her mouth, she knew it was a mistake. He had told her that he didn't intend to work for her. With Chad gone, any job associated with the Legacy would in some way be working for her. That she was now in charge was an idea she hadn't completely embraced.

"As what? Head of the parking-deck security?"

She'd been expecting bitterness and heard only amusement. "That job's still open," she said, answering in kind, "but that *wasn't* what I had in mind."

"Thanks, but something will turn up. It always does."

Clearly an end-of-subject signal. Her desire to make the wrong done to him right prevented her from heeding it.

"My offer wasn't made out of gratitude, if that's what you're thinking."

"Let it go, Kelly."

"You can get kicked out of the Phoenix because of me, risk your life for me, refuse to take any salary for protecting me, but I'm not allowed to offer you a legitimate position."

"That's right," he said pleasantly. He lifted the lid to check the rice.

"Then how about some other form of compensation?" she said, raising her chin defiantly.

She had the satisfaction of seeing his hand hesitate in midair before he carefully set the lid back down and turned to look at her.

"Like what?" His voice was soft and totally controlled.

Her heart had begun to race, either at her daring in making that second offer or in anticipation that he might accept it. Maybe at both.

"I told you that I trusted you to set your own price," she said. "I still do."

Her knees went weak at what was suddenly in his eyes. She had known last night this was probably not a good idea, not with everything that was going on, but it was something she could no longer resist.

All the things that had made her turn to this man, a perfect stranger, on that first night were still in play: instant physical attraction, her loneliness, grief over her brother's death, and a sense that she was being overwhelmed by circumstances. In addition to those, a strong sexual chemistry had been added to the mix.

She knew the kind of man he was. That he could be trusted. That he had integrity and courage and honor.

She also knew the kind of lover he was. Skilled and considerate. Patient and demanding. Exciting.

And she knew that he wanted her. He'd made that obvious last night.

Let me know when it isn't about gratitude. Or an aberration. I'll be around.

"Are you sure?" he asked.

Like Cabot, he believed in cutting to the chase. She couldn't fault him for that.

"The only thing I'm sure about right now is that this isn't about gratitude."

He held her eyes a second longer, assessing. Then those long, dark fingers she had just admired reached across the stove to shut off both burners.

He turned back to her, taking the single step that would bring them face-to-face. Her eyes followed each motion, the sweet, hot ache of desire moving through her lower body.

He took the glass from her unresisting fingers, setting it beside his own before he leaned forward. Her eyes closed as his mouth settled over hers.

With the touch of his lips all the emotions of the night they'd made love came flooding back. Her tongue met his with an eagerness that shocked her. Apparently, the strength of her response surprised him, too.

He deepened the kiss, crushing her to him with a need that seemed as great as hers. His hand slipped beneath the hem of the cotton sweater she was wearing. Warm and firm, slightly callused, his fingers were sensually abrasive as they slid over her skin.

They cupped beneath her breast, applying a pressure that was almost painful. She gasped and immediately it eased.

His mouth continued to ravage, growing more demanding, as his hands found the bottom of her sweater. His lips released, as he stepped far enough back to ease the garment off over her head. He tossed it on the counter. The moisture on her lips hadn't had time to dry before his mouth descended again.

While he kissed her, his fingers made quick work of the hooks at the back of her bra. In a couple of heartbeats it had joined her top on the counter. Then he leaned back, looking down at her.

The first time they'd made love, he had undressed her in the dimness of her bedroom. Afterward he had taken her to bed, where they had been surrounded by the comforting, anonymous darkness. His mouth had explored every inch of her body, but she had never felt exposed. Here in the fluorescent brightness of his kitchen, she did.

His right hand lifted, its fingers almost reverently making contact with the peak of her breast. Despite her awareness of her own nudity, the nipple hardened under his touch. It grew tauter still as his thumb and forefinger closed around the nub, rolling the tender flesh between them.

A wave of longing roared through her body, the feeling so intense that she closed her eyes against its force. Her breath eased out in a long, shuddering sigh.

"You like that?"

She couldn't find the strength to answer him. She nodded instead, and the pressure increased minutely, causing her to draw in the breath she had just released in a jagged inhalation.

"Tell me," he said, his voice softly persuasive.

Unsure if she were capable of forming the words he'd demanded, she forced her eyes open, looking up into his, darkened with a hunger that matched her own.

"Tell me," he urged again.

"I like it," she whispered obediently. "I like it when you touch me."

He nodded as if she were a child who had mastered a difficult lesson. And then his head began to lower once more.

This time his lips closed over the taut nub he had created, their warmth and softness replacing the callused strength of his fingers. He began to suckle her breast, the pressure deep and strong, sending involuntary shivers through her frame.

Her hand found the back of his head, fingers spreading through the thick, dark hair. Holding him to her.

The sensation created by his mouth built until it was almost unbearable, teetering on the fine edge between pleasure and pain. Her fingers tightened, clenching against the force of what he was making her feel.

Just as she thought she could stand it no longer, the suction eased. His tongue rimmed the areola of her nipple, and then he raised his head, blowing lightly against the dampness he'd left on her sensitized skin.

Her breath caught, again shuddering out in response to what he was doing. It seemed that she had been waiting an eternity for his touch. Waiting for him. Wanting him without knowing what she wanted. Now she did.

"And that?" he asked. "Do you like that?"

"You know," she whispered, bending her head until her forehead rested against his. "You know I do."

"I know," he said, the warmth of his breath feathering over her skin. "I know everything about you. I know everything you like. You taught me."

She nodded, her head still resting against his. His tongue laved again, sending a bolt of pure electric pleasure into the bottom of her stomach.

"Not here," he suggested.

She nodded again, mindless with how much she wanted him. She couldn't even remember why she had fought this last night. They were both adults. Both apparently free of emotional encumbrances.

They had been thrown together by circumstances beyond their control. Circumstances that made her dependent on this man for her safety.

Let me know when it isn't about gratitude.

It wasn't, she told herself. She *was* grateful. And she should be. But this…

This was about the way his hands felt trailing over her skin. The way his kiss stole not only her breath, but her will. The memory of being crushed beneath solid, sweat-slick muscle. Of bone pounding against bone as his body lifted and then lowered into hers.

As those images unfolded in her head, he suddenly straightened, leaving her lips bereft. They tried to follow, but he stepped to the side. Taking her arm just above the elbow, he urged her forward, but she couldn't bear to be separated from him even the short time it would take to walk to the bedroom.

"Bedroom," he said, putting his hand against the small of her back to guide her.

She nodded, knowing that he was right. She wanted to savor every sensual detail of their lovemaking. The atmosphere of the kitchen wasn't conducive to that. Much better the dark intimacy of his bedroom.

Giving in to his guidance, she took a step. As she did, her cell phone rang. Her first thought was that she should have made sure it was off. The second was that the call might be from any one of the people she had talked to this afternoon. And that all of them might have information they needed.

"I should answer that," she said.

"Why?" His hand still rested on her back, but he was no longer urging her forward.

"It might be Catherine."

She was the only one who had promised to call, although she hadn't talked as if she had expected it to be today. Maybe she'd gotten lucky. Maybe *they'd* gotten lucky.

Without waiting for his approval, she walked over to the table where she'd set it down with the groceries they'd bought on the way home. The phone had already rung three times by the time she'd fumbled it out of the bag. One more ring, and her voice mail would pick up. Hurriedly she punched the button.

"Hello?"

"Thank goodness I caught you," Catherine said. "I was beginning to believe you were too busy with tall, dark and handsome to answer your phone."

"No, I'm here." Only belatedly did she realize how stupid that was.

"Good. I've got something you need to hear. Grab your watch dog and get over here."

"Tonight?"

"Too good to wait, my dear. I think this is something both of you will be very interested in."

"About what we were talking about this afternoon?"

"Of course."

"About—"

Deliberately she hesitated, hoping Catherine would fill in the blank. She didn't.

"I don't tell secrets on the phone. Especially not on a cell phone. Remember Princess Diana and all the trouble she got in, although they said that was MI5." In the midst of that non sequitur, Catherine seemed to realize she'd gotten off course. "You want the information I've got for you, then you come over here. Otherwise…"

The old woman didn't bother to complete the threat. They both knew it was meaningless. It was obvious she was dying to share whatever she'd learned, but apparently she wanted the drama of their rushing over there to hear it firsthand. And there was always the possibility that she might really have uncovered something they could use. Despite the hyperbole, Catherine did know a hell of a lot of influential people.

"We'll be there in half an hour."

As she said the words, Kelly looked up. Straight into the eyes of the man who, less than a minute ago, had been about to carry her to his bed and make love to her. She pressed the off button on her cell, taking it away from her ear as she did.

"Catherine," she said unnecessarily.

"And she wants us to come over there."

She made a small gesture of helplessness, opening her hands with the palms up.

"She say what it's about?"

"Only that it concerned something we talked about this afternoon."

He released a breath so strong it was audible. Without another word he picked her bra and sweater up off the counter and handed them to her.

"Then what are we waiting for?"

Chapter Seventeen

"You're sure she meant for us to meet her here?"

Kelly had begun to wonder the same thing as they pulled into the driveway of the Suttle home. There were no lights inside or outside the big house.

Of course, that might be intended for their protection. If Catherine had found something as important as she'd indicated on the phone, it would be to their advantage that no one knew about this meeting.

"That's what she said. Maybe she gave the servants the night off because we were coming."

"What do you want to bet that whatever she's discovered, it isn't as earth-shattering as she indicated on the phone? I don't see how she could find out anything all that valuable in the space of a few hours."

"Say what you will about Catherine, she *does* have connections."

"So she told us."

John's skepticism was more healthy than her own rush of adrenaline when she'd heard Catherine's voice. He was right. The old woman liked to flaunt her insider status.

It would be like her to call and get them to come all the way out here just to share some piece of gossip she'd heard, either about a fellow board member or someone supposedly connected to The Covenant. The chances that they'd get something helpful from this visit were slim to none.

"Why don't we go see what she's got?" She put her fingers over the handle of the car door.

"I go first," John instructed. "You stay right behind me. And I mean *right* behind me."

The order drew her eyes to him. He was looking at the mansion in front of them, his profile silhouetted against the moon-touched darkness outside the window.

"You can't possibly think—"

"I think we don't take any chances. You don't call somebody up and invite them over and then leave the place dark as a tomb."

"Unless she thought we'd want it like that," she suggested.

"Or unless this is a setup. Either way, I lead and you follow. *Closely.* I want to be able to put my hand back and touch you at any time."

Although neither his tone nor the situation was in the least suggestive, her body reacted to that choice of words. Probably the result of the situation Catherine's call had interrupted.

John opened the driver's side door, stepping out onto the driveway. He waited a moment, taking a visual scan of their surroundings. Apparently whatever he saw—or didn't see—reassured him.

He walked around the front of the SUV and opened her door, waiting until she climbed out before easing the door back against the frame without really closing it. He had done the same thing with his, making the process as noiseless as possible.

It wasn't until he stepped in front of her that she saw he had taken his gun from its holster. He held the weapon out before him, right hand around the grip, the left steadying it.

As much as possible, he stayed within the shadows cast by the house as he led the way to the front door. Following his instructions, she trailed him so closely that she could have reached out and touched his back. Never once did he turn to check on her progress, trusting she would obey his instructions.

When they reached the entryway, he used his left arm to position her against the wall of the house, putting his body in front of hers. He listened a moment before he reached toward the lighted doorbell button.

Halfway there, his hand stopped, hovering in midair. She leaned forward, trying to see what the holdup was. He turned his head, eyes meeting hers. One dark brow lifted in inquiry.

If something *was* wrong inside the house, ringing the bell probably wasn't the smart thing to do. Catherine was expecting them. She would understand their concerns. She nodded, giving him permission.

His fingers closed around the ornate brass handle of the door. He depressed the lock mechanism with his thumb, and the door swung inward.

Neither of them moved. She held her breath, listening to the eerie stillness inside the house. She could feel coldness from the air-conditioned interior seeping out around them into the humid Georgetown night.

John raised his left hand, gesturing for her to follow. As he did, he moved through the open door into the darkness inside the house.

She took a breath that was intended to be calming. It wasn't. She had the same feeling she'd had the night of the storm when she'd heard the breaking glass. Something wasn't right here.

They wouldn't know what it was unless they entered that cold, silent darkness. And that was the last thing she wanted to do.

I want to be able to put my hand back and touch you....

She had no choice. John was waiting for her inside. And no matter what else was waiting in there, she didn't want to be left alone out here.

She forced her feet to move across the brick entryway, stepping over the threshold without making a sound. It took a second or two for her eyes to adjust to the interior darkness. As they did, a figure emerged before her.

It was John, moving down the entry hall, his weapon still held out before him. She hurried to catch up with him, running soundlessly on tiptoe across the marble foyer.

She had intended to touch to let him know that she was behind him. Before her fingers made contact with his shoulder, she realized that might be a mistake. She lowered her hand, clenching her fingers into a fist to stop their shaking.

Her eyes had become accustomed to the lack of light, enough that she could make out individual pieces of furniture in the rooms they were passing. On the left was the ballroom-size living room where Catherine entertained. On the right was the equally large dining room where a lavish buffet was always set out for her guests. John ignored both, moving steadily toward the back of the house. Heading to the glass-enclosed sitting room where Catherine had led them today?

They had reached the end of the entry hall. Ahead of them was the wide, curving staircase that split at a central landing and then went on up to the second floor. John paused at its foot.

Only the lower portion of the staircase—up to the first landing—was visible. She knew Catherine's suite was on the second floor and to the right, but she could see nothing at the top of the stairs but a thicker darkness. Everything around them was utterly still.

John headed to the left of the stairs, toward the sitting room that had been filled with sunlight this afternoon. He'd apparently come to the same conclusion she'd reached. If Catherine were waiting for them, it would be there.

If Catherine were waiting for them...

The thought was so bizarre that it continued to nag at her as she followed John. Catherine had called and asked them to come. She had told them she had important information. Why *wouldn't* she be waiting for them?

Unaware that John had stopped, she ran into his back. His arm came out, pressing her close to him. Again they listened together. This time she heard what had halted his forward progress. Sounds, indistinct and unidentifiable, were coming from the room where she had believed John was headed.

He turned to look at her over his shoulder. He put his forefinger to his lips and then held up his hand, the palm facing her. She nodded her understanding.

He stepped forward, almost immediately disappearing into the darkness. Back against the wall, she waited, straining to catch any sounds that might give her some clue as to what was happening. It was no use. Not only could she not follow John's progress, but the faint noises that had lured him toward the sitting room seemed to have disappeared.

As she waited in the stillness, her eyes strained for his reappearance in the dark passage before her. She had no idea how long he'd been gone. Even if she had glanced at her watch when he left, she wouldn't have been able to read the hands.

All she knew was that it was too long. Too long without

some sound. Too long without something happening. Certainly too long to explore that relatively small room.

She took a step, keeping her back to the wall. And then another. When she reached the door of the sitting room, perhaps she could see him. The one thing she couldn't do was to continue to stand here without knowing what was happening.

She eased along the wall until she was almost to the entrance. One more step and she would be able to see into the room. Already she could perceive a brightness there, the expanse of glass allowing the moon to bathe the room with filtered light.

There was still no sound. Nothing to indicate what was happening beyond that opening.

Gathering her courage, she took the final step that would align her with the arched doorway. The cream-colored couch drew her eyes first, and then they scanned the other objects in the room.

Objects and not people. Wherever John had disappeared to, it was obvious he wasn't here. And if he wasn't, then where was he?

She turned her head, looking back at the place where he'd told her to wait. Compared to the sitting room, the hallway seemed darker than when she'd been standing there. She didn't want to retrace her steps, moving into what had now become the unknown. Far better to go forward into the light than back into that blackness.

The sitting room beckoned invitingly. At least there she would be able to see who or what was around her.

She took a final glance down the hallway, hoping to find John emerging from its shadows. Then, without allowing herself time to think about what she was doing, she took the step that would carry her under the arch and into the room where Catherine had offered them tea this afternoon.

The garden beyond the wide windows and French doors was lost in patterns of shade and deeper shadow. There was nothing moving out there. On the other side of the room was a narrow door that had been closed this afternoon. Now it was open. From what she remembered about the layout of the house, that passage led to the kitchen and the servants' quarters.

Since John hadn't come back through the arch and since the garden outside appeared deserted, she started across the expanse of white carpeting. As she neared the end of the damask-covered sofa, something caught her eye. Between the couch and the chair where Catherine had perched today, something long and dark marred the pale carpeting.

John? The crumpled shape was too small. Too narrow.

She arrived at the identification long before her conscious mind was willing to accept it. Catherine Suttle lay on her expensive wool carpeting, pale blue eyes open and staring up at the plaster medallion in the center of the room.

Trembling, Kelly took the final step that would bring her to the side of the woman who had been her friend and confidante since she'd arrived in Washington. She knelt, reaching out to touch the long patrician fingers that rested against the silk dressing gown Catherine was wearing. The diamonds that adorned them still glittered in the moonlight.

There was no sign of injury. No blood. Except for the glazed eyes, the old woman might have been asleep.

A heart attack? Or a stroke?

Despite the attempts that had been made on her own life, it took a moment for the possibility that someone had killed Catherine to penetrate her shock. When it did, she realized that the woman who had asked her to come here, a woman who had claimed to have some vital information to give her, was dead.

And that the man who had promised to protect her was nowhere to be found.

DESPITE THE FACT that he hadn't paused more than a couple of seconds to examine Catherine's body, the dark shape John had caught out of the corner of his eye as he'd entered the sitting room was nowhere to be seen. The hallway into which he'd followed his quarry had ended in a cramped stairwell that led to a lower level.

There he'd discovered a labyrinth of narrow passages and small, windowless rooms, obviously the remnants of the servants' domain from the turn of the century. His search had been slowed by the necessary examination of each, leaving him feeling like a rat in a maze.

Every second he spent peering through the darkness, hoping to stumble across whoever had been in the house with Catherine when they arrived, he was aware that Kelly was alone. Once before, the night she had seen the intruder in the shower, he'd been forced to make this same decision. He'd chosen then not to put her at risk in order to pursue the man in the ski mask. As a result of that choice, another woman was now dead.

Once and for all, the continuing threat to her safety had to be confronted. Since the figure he'd seen had been moving in front of him, he hadn't overly worried about leaving Kelly upstairs. However, as the minutes ticked off while he moved deeper and deeper into the oldest part of the mansion, there was a growing sense that she'd been unprotected too long.

There was also the remote possibility that the conclusion he'd drawn from his hurried examination of the old woman had been wrong. Maybe she hadn't been dead. In that case she needed immediate medical attention. And it was obvious with each passing second that he wasn't going to find the person he'd been chasing down here.

Frustrated that the killer had once more been within his grasp and escaped, he began to retrace his steps. He kept the Glock in position in case his prey had found a hiding place and was waiting for him to do exactly what he was doing.

Despite his anticipation of an ambush, he reduced his original journey, which, delayed by the search, had taken several long minutes, to less than five. As he entered the sitting room, his eyes immediately focused on the woman who still lay on the white carpet.

He walked over to Catherine and, bending down, put his fingers over the carotid artery. He waited, but there could be no doubt this time. The life-giving pulse of blood was still.

Catherine Suttle had been wrong. The bastards, whichever ones she'd meant, *had* messed with her.

He reached up and placed the tips of his fingers on the crepe-like eyelids, pulling them down to cover the glazed eyes. She looked more at peace now. As if she were sleeping in the moonlight.

He stood, turning toward the arched entryway and the hall where he'd left Kelly. Given the time that had passed, he would have thought she'd be in the sitting room by now, but apparently she had followed his directions.

As he stepped through the arch, the darkness in the hall was stygian compared to the sitting room. It took a moment for his eyes to adjust. As they did, he realized that it wasn't that he hadn't been able to see Kelly in the darkness. The problem was that she was no longer waiting where he'd left her.

Chapter Eighteen

The hand that had fastened over her mouth was covered with a thin leather glove. She could smell the distinctive fragrance of the tanned hide it had been made of. She could also smell the man who was holding her.

The acrid tang of tension-induced perspiration underlay the scent of the cologne or aftershave he was wearing. Something subtle and expensive. Despite her fears, she had immediately realized the significance of that.

The first time he had hired someone to do his dirty work. The kids in the parking deck had reeked of stale cigarettes and dirty T-shirts. This was the smell of Wall Street on a bad day. That didn't make it any less terrifying.

Upset with finding Catherine's body, she had not been paying enough attention. Her first thought had been that she should try to find John, but given the size and darkness of the house, she'd quickly realized that wandering off in search of him was asking for the kind of scenario that had, ironically, just taken place.

Instead of accepting the beckoning door on the far side of the sitting room, she had started back toward the hall where John had told her to wait. She'd planned to go out to the car and call the police on her cell phone, but she hadn't gotten that far.

The man who was now holding her had been standing in the shadows as she came through the arch. The blow to the back of her head had not caused her to lose consciousness. At least she didn't think it had. Her knees had buckled with the force of it, however, throwing her to the floor.

As she lay there helpless, a wet rag or a handkerchief had been shoved under her nose. Whatever it was soaked with burned her nostrils and clouded her mind, so that although she was somehow aware that her wrists were being tied behind her back, she didn't even struggle.

He had hoisted her to her feet by putting his hands under her armpits and dragging her up. Before she could manage to put her thoughts together, his fingers had clamped over her lips, and the cold, hard muzzle of his gun had been pressed against her neck.

"Make a sound and you're dead," he'd whispered, his lips against her ear.

Compliant through a combination of pain, shock and the effects of the substance on the rag, she had stumbled backward under his guidance. All she could think about was why he didn't just shoot her. It took her too long to understand that he couldn't without calling attention to their location. And longer still to grasp the significance of his reluctance to do so.

John was alive.

Only with the flood of eye-stinging relief did she realize how terrified she had been that he might not be. If he were, he would come for her. She knew that with a certainty that allowed no doubt, not even in the face of her terror. Just as he had faced down those teenagers that first night, John would find and neutralize the threat posed by the man who held her prisoner in the shadows underneath the staircase.

They waited together, their breathing suspended as they listened for any noise made by the only other living soul in this house. She closed her eyes, sending a silent prayer heavenward on his behalf.

At least she was again able to think. The pain that had stunned and sickened her was easing to a dull hammering, and even the aftereffects of those paralyzing fumes were fading. As they did, her vision started to clear.

From the darkness under the stairs, she could see the hallway that led to the sitting room. At any moment now—

Suddenly, almost a revelation, she realized that as soon as John appeared in his field of vision, the man holding the gun would turn the muzzle away from her and shoot him. Then he would finish the job he'd begun by killing her.

There was no reason not to. No reason to discuss or negotiate. Simply by believing that everything from Chad's death to Catherine Suttle's revolved around the allocation of the Lockett Legacy monies, she knew enough to be dangerous to this man's plans.

She began to squirm, trying to free her mouth from the gloved hand so she could warn John. It was no use. The man's grip had been firm and painful. As she struggled, it tightened cruelly. His fingers now covered her nostrils in an attempt to frighten her into submission.

Instead, the lack of air reinforced her sense that this was the last chance either of them had. She had to make some sound, even if it were an inarticulate grunt. At least then John would have some warning that something was wrong.

She began to moan, the noise coming from deep within her throat. She continued to try to twist her head away from the controlling hand, hoping that she could get her lips open to scream, if only for a fraction of a second.

"I swear I'll kill you," the man behind her hissed, his breath hot on her cheek. "You make another sound, and I'll blow your brains out. *That'll* get him out here."

To prove his point, he moved the gun up, jamming it

against her temple. The shock of the threat and the realization that he was right silenced her. In the sudden stillness she could hear a noise beside her ear as if he had cocked the weapon.

And then, almost simultaneously, she heard footsteps. Someone was coming down the marble hallway from the direction of the sitting room.

MAYBE KELLY HAD GONE OUT to the car. As they'd left his apartment, she'd put the cell phone Catherine had called her on into her purse, which she'd left on the front seat of the SUV. If she *had* come into the sitting room and seen the body—

He would never know what made him hesitate. Instinct. Experience. Some unidentifiable sound or a half-seen movement in the depth of the shadows at the end of the hall.

Whatever it was, it saved his life. The bullet slammed into the wall beside him, exactly where he would have been had he not stopped. Before its echo had faded from the confined space, he was back on the other side of the arch.

It was impossible to return fire since he had no idea where Kelly was. Until he had located her...

"Kelly?" he called, hoping against hope that she'd be able to answer him.

Instead, another shot exploded into the wooden frame of the arch, shattering it. He flinched, closing his eyes and throwing up a protective arm to shield his eyes from the splinters.

"Drop it," a voice from his right ordered.

Wrong direction. Wrong voice. Wrong sex. He began to turn, but the added warning stopped the movement.

"With you dead, she won't have any chance at all, and you know it. Drop the gun."

His peripheral vision was good enough that, guided by sound, he could distinguish a dark shape in the doorway on the other side of the room. There were two of them, then. Both armed. Given their positions, they could keep him pinned down by a deadly crossfire.

And whoever the speaker was, she was right. If they shot him, there would be nothing—and no one—to keep them from killing Kelly. That had obviously been their intent from the beginning.

It wasn't as if he had a hell of a lot of options right now. If he turned enough to put him into a position to get off a shot at the woman, then whoever was at the end of the hall would put a bullet into his back or his head. The only choice he couldn't afford to make was one that would result in his immediate death. That might come later, but right now—

Moving carefully, he bent his knees, lowering his weapon to lay it on the floor. As he stood up again, he raised his hands in the classic gesture of surrender. His stomach was clenched into a knot, waiting for the impact of a bullet to his gut.

"Kick it out into the hall," the female voice demanded.

He hesitated for a fraction of a second, again weighing his chances. Then he edged the Glock around with his toe and shoved it with his foot into the dark hallway.

"It's okay," the woman yelled to her companion before she lowered her voice to address him. "Sit on the couch," she directed as she crossed the room toward him. "And keep your hands where I can see them."

By now he had recognized the voice. Bertha Reynolds had obviously seen too many gangster movies through the years. The old-fashioned kind where people talked while they held guns on other people.

Of course, corny dialogue had a distinct advantage over

the more realistic versions of how this situation should play out. As long as she was talking, nothing bad was happening.

"So nice of you to join us," Bertha said, her eyes flicking to the doorway.

John looked away from the muzzle of the big Walther she was holding in both hands to find Kelly being ushered in under the arch. Despite the darkness, her captor had again opted for the ski mask. The combination of the gun against Kelly's temple and his sinister appearance reminded John that, despite Bertha's age, two people had already died at their hands.

"On the couch," the man said.

Not Daniels. His was the one voice John was sure he would have recognized. There was no trace of that smooth Southern drawl.

The man shoved Kelly forward forcefully so that she staggered toward the sofa. John met her eyes, shaking his head to let her know not to try anything. The memory of her desperately attacking those kids with only a sandal had begun to haunt him. Of course, with her hands tied behind her back, there was little she could do.

Almost as an unwanted answer to that comforting thought, Bertha instructed her associate, "Untie her."

The question the order raised led to only one answer. They needed Kelly to do something that involved the use of her hands. Whatever that was explained why they were still alive.

Untying Kelly seemed to give them an unexpected advantage. If he could only figure out how to use it.

"Why are you doing this?" Kelly asked as the man in the mask loosened the strips of cloth with which he'd bound her wrists. That seemed a strange choice, but maybe they'd had to improvise.

"Money, my dear. A lot of it," Bertha answered.

"The Legacy."

"For which we have better uses than you or Chad could have devised."

The man stuffed the bindings in the pocket of his pants before he pushed Kelly forward again. As she eased down on the couch beside him, John caught a whiff of chloroform. Not an impromptu attack, then. Or maybe they had brought it to use on Catherine.

"Keep them covered."

Bertha moved sideways, her own weapon still focused on John. She reached down beside one of the two wing chairs that faced the sofa and retrieved an oversize purse. She must have come to visit Catherine openly and then, with the assistance of the guy in the mask, overpowered her, taking the older woman by surprise.

Maybe she had been the one who had provided the "information" Catherine had been so excited about. If so, the ploy had worked. Both on Catherine and on them.

Bertha took a sheaf of papers from the bag and, without taking her eyes or her weapon off him, she walked forward to lay the documents on the coffee table in front of Kelly. She straightened, stepping back with the same vigilance she'd maintained from the first. Whatever else she might be, she wasn't careless.

"There are two places for you to sign. Both are marked with an X. X marks the spot," Bertha said almost jovially. "Just like a treasure hunt. Actually, the analogy isn't far off."

It was obvious she was feeling expansive. Maybe he could use that to buy some time. In those black-and-white films she'd obviously learned her dialogue from, villains always talked too much.

"With the Legacy as the treasure," he suggested.

She moved to consider his face. "A well-established, very legitimate and *very* high-profile organization. One that was already giving away millions a year and, with the right guidance, has the potential to generate many more."

"And yours is the right guidance, I suppose." Kelly's comment, laced with sarcasm, quickly brought the woman's focus back to her. "Couldn't you convince Chad to do what you wanted?"

"Your brother had the unfortunate notion that the final decisions should all be his. And he asked inconvenient questions. I'm afraid I saw the same tendencies in you, my dear. We weren't about to play that game again."

"We being The Covenant?" John asked. "Or we being the two of you?"

"Semantics," Bertha said, ignoring the opening he'd given her. "We had goals for the money that Chad so tirelessly raised. When he became difficult, however…"

"You killed him," Kelly said, her voice full of loathing.

"Of course not," Bertha said. "It was pilot error. Caused by an overdose of medication. Didn't someone explain all that to you? By the way, just in case you're wondering, that *will* be the official outcome of the inquiry."

"How can you know that?" John asked.

"Because there are some very powerful people involved in this. If Cabot continues to investigate, he may find he's bitten off even more than he can chew."

"Don't underestimate him." If anything happened to them, he found it comforting to think that the Phoenix was already interested in the plans of these two. And in The Covenant.

"Underestimating people is a mistake I seldom make. Except in her case, I suppose. Congratulations, my dear. I was sure you'd be exactly as Chad viewed you."

"What does that mean?"

"Someone who had little use for her family's wealth and even less use for life in Washington. We thought you'd make the requisite appearance after Chad's death and then turn the governance of the Legacy over to the board."

"Sorry to disappoint you."

"Oh, it will all work out in the end," Bertha assured her. "It's even better this way. You sign control of the foundation over to the directors, we won't have to worry about anyone's interference with it ever again."

"I wouldn't count on that," John said.

"Cabot? Without Kelly paying him, I would imagine he'll be more than willing to let this drop."

"Actually, the Phoenix's interest in the Legacy began long before Kelly approached them."

Bertha's hesitation in responding told him what he had wanted to know. She hadn't known Cabot's involvement predated Kelly's visit to his office. Apparently The Covenant wasn't as omniscient as they liked to believe.

Bertha's eyes shifted to her partner's face. John's muscles had already tensed in preparation for action when she quickly brought her attention back to him. Although the time when she hadn't been watching him had been very brief, he cursed himself for not taking advantage of the opportunity. He might not get another. Things seemed to be winding down, the woman no longer inclined to brag about their cleverness.

His comments about Griff and the Phoenix had bothered her. She was ready to get this over and move on to crisis control. If Kelly signed that document, she would be signing their death warrant.

"Sufficient unto the day," Bertha said piously. "We'll deal with Cabot. And believe me, no matter how well connected he thinks he is, he doesn't stand a chance."

"I'll tell him that. I'm sure he'll lose sleep over it."

"You think you're so bright. All of you. Intellectual snobbery in its worst incarnation. You had one lousy job to do for this country, and you couldn't even do that properly."

It took a second or two to fit the accusation into the context of their conversation. When he had, it seemed as bizarre as everything else about Bertha Reynolds holding a gun on them.

"All you had to do was protect us," she went on, "and you couldn't manage it. Then our vaunted military couldn't track down those who were responsible."

Her voice had grown shriller as her diatribe continued. The gun was still leveled at them, but he could sense that her mind was more on what she was saying, apparently a familiar rant, than on watching them.

"Well, pretty soon you won't have any options," she continued. "The American people are finally going to rise up and demand that the earth be purged of those infidels. We're going to see to that."

As insane as the threat was, he was beginning to get an inkling of The Covenant's connection to terrorism. No wonder no one had been able to figure out what was going on. The logic was so twisted it defied rationality.

"Jihad," he said. "And you're inciting it."

"There's never been a more *holy* war in the course of human history," the woman said. "And this time we'll be the ones waging it."

"But first you have to show everyone how real the threat is."

"People in this town don't act. They only react."

"So you fund a little domestic terrorism to cause the reaction you want."

"Bertha." For the first time the man in the ski mask spoke, his tone conveying a warning.

"Hugh? Hugh, is that you?"

Kelly's voice indicated the shock of her recognition. Of course, as head of accounting for the Legacy, Donaldson was in a perfect position to carry out Bertha's bizarre fantasy. That the CEO of a major American company could believe this holy war crap was far harder to swallow.

There was no answer to Kelly's question, although the man she'd identified as Hugh Donaldson took his eyes off them long enough to glance toward the woman holding the Walther. Again John wondered if he should take that infinitesimal chance to launch an attack. Before he could turn thought into action, Donaldson's weapon had steadied.

"And after Kelly signs the foundation over to your control? What will you do then?" John asked, trying to provoke another moment of inattention or rage. "The body count is building. It's going to be increasingly hard to explain. First Chad. Then Catherine." Deliberately he looked down at the old woman, lying almost at his feet. "The two of us. Don't you think that eventually someone's going to notice?"

"Why should they? Chad died because of pilot error. An unfortunate diabetic coma claimed Catherine's life, ironically on a night she'd sent her servants away. And poor Kelly Lockett," Bertha said, her voice unctuous, "still distraught over her brother's death, takes her own life."

It was the scenario he'd imagined when they found the broken glass in Chad's kitchen. It even explained the cloth bindings. Less likely to leave marks that might make the medical examiner question a finding of suicide.

"Sorry to disappoint you, Bertha," Kelly said. "I'm not signing your damned papers. You must be insane if you think I'll make it that easy for you. If I'm going to die anyway—"

"What about him?" Bertha asked, pointed the Walther at John's midsection. "Would you sign them if he begged you to? How about if we start with a kneecap."

"Blood splatters on Catherine's carpet will be hard to explain away," John said.

In spite of that bravado, a growing coldness invaded his gut. Kelly was right. Bertha Reynolds *was* insane. They both must be to think they could get away with this.

"This is Catherine's gun. If we have to, we'll put it in her hand—"

The words cut off abruptly as a melodious chime echoed through the dark house. Someone was ringing the front bell.

Chapter Nineteen

It was the chance he had been waiting for. John lunged forward, trying to wrest the gun from Bertha's hand before it went off. As he'd expected, she pulled the trigger as soon as she realized what he was after. He managed to push the muzzle slightly to the side, far enough that the bullet struck one of the windows behind him, shattering glass.

His momentum carried him into her, throwing her to the floor. The gun struck the carpet and skittered away in the darkness. As he crawled across Bertha, trying to locate the weapon, Donaldson finally reacted.

Despite the dimness of the moonlit room, the accountant's aim was accurate. If John hadn't been scrambling for the gun, the bullet would have hit him in the back. Instead, it struck Bertha Reynolds, who was still pinned beneath his legs. He heard her gasp at the impact, a sharp inhalation, followed by a low moaning release.

By that time his searching fingers had located the Walther. He secured it, turning onto his back even as his hands locked into the familiar position around the grip. The third bullet struck the floor beside him, missing him by centimeters. Torso lifted and head up, he could now see the other occupants of the room.

Kelly had come up off the couch while he was searching

for Bertha's weapon. She was clinging to Donaldson's arm, trying to prevent him from getting off another shot. The accountant attempted to push her away, but she held on for dear life. *Literally.*

As they struggled, their bodies shifted from side to side. Their positions probably varied no more than inches in either direction, but those were enough to keep John from risking a shot.

Suddenly Donaldson shoved Kelly violently away from him, causing her to lose her balance. She stumbled against the table at the end of the sofa. The muzzle of the gun in Donaldson's hand began to track her progress.

Maybe he believed that since John hadn't returned fire, he was either incapacitated or had been unable to find Bertha's weapon. It was his last mistake.

No longer hindered by a fear of hitting Kelly, John pulled the trigger. Donaldson staggered backward a couple of steps, as if driven by the impact of the bullet, before he collapsed.

John was on his feet before the other man hit the carpet. As soon as he was sure Bertha was no longer a threat, he crossed to Kelly, putting his hand under her elbow to help her up. Then he slipped his arm around her waist, urging her toward the archway that led into the hall.

They owed their lives to whoever had rung the bell. In spite of the reaction of their captors to its sound, however, there was no guarantee the person at the door was a friend.

John paused at the arch, pushing Kelly behind him as he carefully peered around its frame into the dark hall. A man, weapon drawn, stood in the shadows beside the moonlit rectangle of the open door.

"John?"

Ethan Snow. It even made sense that he was here. He had taken over the case, and Cabot's orders from the first had been to keep an eye on Kelly Lockett. Thankfully, Ethan *had* been tonight.

"It's over. We're okay," he assured the Phoenix agent.

"No mopping up to be done?"

"Not the kind you mean," John acknowledged, thinking of the political implications of all this as well as of the physical carnage in the sitting room. "But probably more of the other than any of us can imagine right now."

"AN ATTEMPT to provoke *us* into a holy war?" Ethan asked, trying to clarify what John had told him.

The police had arrived, and the technicians were processing the scene, using lighting they'd brought in. The three of them had been asked to stay at the house until they could go over the whole thing again with the detectives. Although Ethan had called Cabot, the head of the Phoenix hadn't put in an appearance yet.

They had chosen to wait in Catherine Suttle's kitchen. Kelly had located some utility candles, which created a dim island of light at the breakfast bar where she was sitting.

"As ridiculous as it sounds, that's what Bertha Reynolds claimed," John said.

"They planned to use money from the Legacy to fund acts of terrorism and lay the blame on the Muslim world," Kelly added.

If it hadn't been for John's actions tonight, they might have succeeded. They had no compunction in eliminating anyone who stood in their way. Chad. Even poor Catherine. And they wouldn't have hesitated to kill her even if she had refused to sign their papers.

Of course, the threat they'd used to try to force her to do that had been highly effective. She would never have been able to watch them shoot John. The worst moment of her life, rivaling the news of Chad's death, had been when

Hugh had fired as John tried to take Bertha's gun. If anything had happened to him—

"That's why there were references to the Legacy in the traffic you intercepted."

Kelly pulled her mind away from the thought of losing John by forcing herself to concentrate on his explanation.

"And you think this ties to The Covenant?" Snow asked. "That's going to be a hard sell."

"Maybe they weren't involved," she suggested. "Donaldson handled the accounting. Maybe he used them for a front for what he was doing with the Legacy money."

"Too bad neither of them survived to answer questions," Ethan said.

"*Questioning* wasn't a high priority at the time."

John's eyes touched on hers as he said it, conveying a message she couldn't mistake. The threat from Donaldson had been to her, and he had wasted no time in eliminating it, even though he had known that the man he was targeting might be an important witness in unraveling whatever had been going on.

"I'm not sure I said thanks," John said to Snow. "Ringing the bell made them let their guard down enough for me to try for one of the weapons."

"I decided something wasn't right. The house was dark, and the two of you had been in here a long time."

"Let's just say that I'm glad you were the one assigned to this particular surveillance."

"I'd like to add my gratitude," Kelly said, "although I think Mr. Cabot can carry on whatever investigation he wants on this without having me watched from now on."

"I'll take that under advisement," Griff said.

They turned to find the head of Phoenix being escorted into the kitchen by one of the uniforms. His dark eyes seemed piercing even by candlelight. They lingered on

John's face longer than on hers or Ethan's, so that Kelly wondered if he were beginning to question his assessment of the man he'd dismissed.

"I take it none of you were injured," Griff said.

"Thanks to John."

Cabot's head tilted as if he were considering her statement. "It's fortunate you have him in your employ."

"He isn't working for me. *Not* that I didn't offer."

"Actually, if it hadn't been for Ethan's arrival—" John began, only to be cut off.

"A mutual admiration society," Cabot said. "In any case, I'm glad no one was hurt."

"Except Reynolds and Donaldson," Ethan reminded him. Apparently he had given a brief outline of tonight's events during the phone call.

"You took both of them out?" Cabot said, turning to John.

"Only Donaldson. He shot the woman while trying for me. Kelly botched his aim."

Cabot raised his brows. "Perhaps I should consider employing Ms. Lockett."

"I'm sure that would make neither of us happy," she said. "Like John, I tend to react to the situation. I believe it's called thinking for yourself."

"To be fair, there was more involved in John's dismissal than a tendency to 'think for himself.'"

Despite her chiding tone, Cabot's response seemed amused rather than angered. But then, he hadn't overreacted to her threat to call the police when she'd believed John had stolen the files from Chad's office. Nor to her comment about removing the surveillance he'd ordered on her. Maybe it was worth taking a chance on telling him the truth.

"You're talking about the night he spent with me."

Cabot inclined his head in agreement, his eyes displaying the same hint of amusement his voice had held.

"Would it do any good to tell you that was at my instigation?"

"I expect my agents to resist temptation, Ms. Lockett," Cabot said, smiling at her. "Even one so great as you."

"Actually, I didn't leave him much choice. It was a strapless red evening gown that required very little in the way of underpinnings," she said, careful not to look at John.

He had claimed that he couldn't go back to the Phoenix, but Ethan was right. Seeing him in action tonight, she had known he belonged with the organization, doing exactly what he had done for her. Helping others through a maze of danger they didn't have the skills to negotiate on their own.

Attempting to stifle a smile, Cabot looked down at the toes of his expensive loafers. When he lifted his head a few seconds later, the grin had been controlled.

"It seems you have a champion," he said to John.

"Not an unbiased opinion," John answered, meeting Cabot's eyes openly.

"Certainly not after you saved my life tonight," Kelly said before she turned her attention to Griff. "Only the most recent of the several occasions on which he's done that. It takes a big man to admit he made a mistake, Mr. Cabot."

"Ethan?" Griff's question seemed out of context, but apparently Snow understood it.

"I've felt from the beginning that John belongs with the Phoenix."

"So your vote is that I was wrong."

Cabot's inflection made it clear he wasn't asking a question. Ethan answered him, anyway.

"Your concern has to be with the team. As an operative, mine is who I want guarding my back in any given situation."

"It depends on what you value most in the people who work for you," Kelly said. "Blind obedience or the ability to weigh a situation and make a decision."

"That's an oversimplification," John said, his eyes again meeting Cabot's.

"Maybe," she admitted. "Especially if he's more interested in lockstep than in results."

"Or maybe *he* underestimated your determination," Griff said, mockingly retaining the third person pronoun she'd been using. "My apologies, Ms. Lockett. I didn't realize how persuasive you could be. Even *without* a red dress."

"If you're going to put him back doing surveillance, he isn't interested," she warned, sensing that she'd won. Or rather that John had.

Now that she'd achieved her objective, there was an inexplicable feeling of regret. Having seen the kind of risks he would undertake working for Cabot, she couldn't help but wonder if it would have been better if she'd left well enough alone. John might have found something that wasn't so dangerous. She might even have convinced him to come to work for the foundation.

Of course, that presumed two things, both of which were in doubt: that she would continue to be involved in the Legacy and that she had that kind of influence on John Edmonds. After all, she hadn't even been able to convince him to let her pay him a salary for protecting her.

"Is that true?" Cabot asked.

John's hesitation lasted through several heartbeats. One part of her wanted him to refuse the Phoenix position altogether. Another part, less selfish, hoped that Cabot would be satisfied that John had served a long enough penance for his supposed sins.

"There's no question that I'd like the same kind of assignments you trusted me with in the beginning. Primarily because I value your trust. I always have. But...I want to be part of what you're doing. I'll do whatever it takes to arrange that."

"I think you just have," Griff said.

He held out his hand, and John put his into it. There was an undercurrent of emotion neither man gave outward expression to. When the handshake ended, Cabot turned to her.

"I'd like to ask you to put your request on hold for the time being."

"My request?"

"Until we find out if anyone else on the foundation's board is involved in this, I'd like to have someone keep an eye on you. For your protection, of course. John has said he's willing to do more surveillance, so..."

"You want to assign him to protect me."

"At least that way he'll get paid."

This time she worked at controlling her own smile. And she made them both wait a couple of seconds for her answer. She could see surprise in John's eyes that she didn't accept immediately.

"Oh," she said, as if a light had dawned. "You mean *money*."

"Any perks that might come with the job are beyond my control," Cabot said without missing a beat. "In the meantime, we'll continue our investigation of The Covenant and the possibility that it might be involved in the diversion of the Legacy. John's free to help with that if he wishes, but his prime responsibility will be to see that you're safe. You are planning on staying in the area, aren't you?"

"I have a business in Connecticut," she said, thinking about how peaceful her life had been before all this. *And how lonely.* "Until my brother's affairs are settled and his name cleared and I can be sure the Legacy is in good hands, however, I won't be going back to it."

Cabot nodded as if he'd expected no less. "I take it you're agreeable to undertaking this particular assignment?" he asked John.

"I couldn't ask for a better one," he said, his eyes on hers.

"Tired?" John asked as he used her key to unlock the front door.

She *was* tired, she realized. Exhausted. Since the phone call about the disappearance of Chad's plane, she hadn't had a moment's peace.

Except for those few hours she had slept in this man's arms, she acknowledged. Somehow she had known from that first night he was someone she could trust. Her instincts hadn't been wrong. Her intellect had simply taken some time to catch up with them.

"Tired and relieved," she said, watching him punch the code into the security pad. "I know what Cabot said, but I can't believe anyone else on the board bought into that insanity. We know Catherine wasn't involved. I can't see any of the others being involved, either. After all, they all campaigned vigorously for their own causes."

Of course, so had Bertha and Hugh. It had been part of their cover. As had their assurances that they'd objected to Chad about the funding change.

She would never believe that he'd known what was going on. When he had discovered how much of the money was being diverted, he would have automatically contacted Hugh. They were probably counting on that.

"Griff and Ethan will get to the bottom of it," John said, following her as she led the way toward Chad's office. "If there are others, there's bound to be some indication, either in their backgrounds or their associations. Believe me, no one is better at tracking down that kind of evidence than the Phoenix. They still have strong ties to the intelligence community. In a case like this, they'll call in a lot of favors."

"It's hard to believe the money Chad raised would be used to hurt people. That was the absolute opposite of what he stood for. He only wanted to do good."

"At least you can be assured it won't be misused any longer."

"I've been thinking about that. When I first came to Washington, I couldn't wait to turn everything over to someone else. To escape a responsibility I had never wanted." She paused, thinking about the commitment she was about to propose.

"And now?"

"I realize how easily it can be corrupted. How many people would be more than willing to use Chad's dream, and the Legacy, for their own ends. I'm not sure I can ever trust anyone else to protect it."

"No one but you, you mean." There was no surprise in his voice.

"It's just that I know so little about what it takes to run an organization like this."

"You know more than you did two months ago. The hard part's over. It has to be easier from now on."

"Assuming no one else is trying to kill me," she said, lightening her tone deliberately.

"Assuming you let *me* worry about that."

"Does that fall under the category of 'Don't worry your pretty little head'?" she asked with a smile.

"I think it's under the 'I'm not about to let anything happen to you' category."

"Good," she said softly. "I have a lot of things left that I want to do with my life."

"Getting the Legacy back on track," he suggested.

"Among others."

"Like my career," he said.

"That was easy. It was obvious Cabot was having second thoughts."

"I think the bit about the red dress convinced him."

"It convinced you, didn't it?" She closed the distance between them, smiling up into his eyes.

"In my case, I think it was the sandal."

"I'm glad you didn't *really* need my help. I would have made a pitiful ally," she said with a laugh.

"And tonight," he went on, his serious tone in contrast to hers. "Disrupting Donaldson's aim. Actually, I can't think of anyone I'd rather have at my back in a fight."

It was a ridiculous statement, which she was sure he knew as well as she did. That it was absurd didn't keep her eyes from filling with tears.

Seeing them, John lifted his hand, intending to wipe away the moisture. Embarrassed, she ducked her head a little to avoid it. He changed the gesture, using his thumb to lift her chin.

He was smiling at her. Acceptance. And something else. Something that beckoned her like the warmth of a fire on a winter's night.

She moved into his arms as naturally as if she had been doing it for years. It felt as though she had.

He looked down into her eyes a long time before his head began to lower. Her lips parted as her eyelids fell, preparing for his kiss. When his mouth fastened over hers, there was again that sense of rightness. Of belonging.

His hand at the base of her spine urged her body closer to his. So close that she could feel the strength of his erection, filling her with an excitement that grew as the kiss deepened.

She couldn't remember why she had resisted this. Tonight there was no hesitation. And no doubts. She belonged in his arms, and it seemed as if her heart had known that from the first.

"Bed," he suggested softly, his lips moving away from hers only enough to utter that single syllable.

And then, taking her agreement for granted, he bent to put his arm beneath her knees, lifting her as he had the night of the auction. There was no trepidation. She was instead filled with joy and anticipation and a sense of coming home after a long and difficult journey.

Epilogue

There was no slow seduction this time. They came together in a frenzy of need. As if facing death had made them more conscious of the sanctity of life. As if some primitive compulsion propelled them toward the most life-affirming act in nature.

Despite the demands John made on her body, he never left her behind. With his hands and lips and tongue he had banished whatever inhibitions she felt, drawing her ever deeper into the web of his desire.

After a few minutes she was no longer conscious of her surroundings. Or of what had happened earlier tonight. She knew only what he could make her feel. And what she felt for him.

He had come into her life at a time when there was no stability within it. From the chaos of loss and fear and danger, he had created a haven of safety in his arms. Because of that, no matter what he asked of her, she knew she could trust him to take care of her.

His hands soothed her tension, replacing it with a growing sense of her own needs that only he could answer. When he began to move above her, controlling his desire in order to carry her with him, the same response she had felt the first night he'd made love to her stirred again. Like a match to tinder, his deep thrusts nurtured the flame within her body. Heat shimmered along nerve pathways, awakening them to the purpose for which they had been created.

Her hands gripped his shoulders, holding him to her as his hips continued to drive above her. When the first tremor began inside, the tips of her fingers bit into the hard muscles beneath her hands, urging him on.

By then the cataclysm was beyond her control. Her body arched and trembled under the relentless demands of his. She was aware when his release joined hers, feeling the hot jetting of his seed and hearing the guttural outcry that signaled his climax. Mindless, powerless, all she could do was hold him to her, as they rode the crest together.

Gradually the assault on her senses eased. Her mind, which had been incapable of thought only seconds before, returned to rationality. To an awareness of his strength. And his gentleness.

She ran the palm of her hand over the perspiration-glazed skin of his back and felt him shiver, either in response to her touch or in a delayed reaction to the power of the climax they had just shared. He rolled onto his side, propping himself up on one elbow to look down at her.

Almost too sated to move, she lifted her hand to run her fingers through his hair, cool and silken against her heated skin. He smiled at her.

"You cried the first time I made love to you."

"Did I?" she asked, repositioning her hand so that her palm framed his cheek. "I don't remember."

"I thought I'd hurt you. Or that you were sorry you'd let me stay."

"I wasn't sorry, but…I confess to second thoughts."

"And now?"

"No second thoughts," she said, running her thumb

across the fullness of his bottom lip. "No thoughts at all. That's what I wanted that night."

She had forgotten what she'd felt then, until he mentioned the tears. She had wanted to be rendered mindless. To forget her grief. And she had desperately wanted not to be alone.

Other than that one tearful moment, he had succeeded in giving her all that she'd needed. Just as he had tonight.

Of course, the emotions that had propelled their first lovemaking had no role in what had happened between them here. This hadn't been about loneliness or isolation. This had been about the two of them.

"Did it work?" he asked. His lips pursed as he kissed her thumb.

"Until the next morning," she said, smiling into his eyes. His were serious—too serious—creating a frisson of unease.

"What's wrong?" she asked, fighting that surge of anxiety.

It seemed that everything had finally been brought to resolution for both of them. She couldn't imagine why he wouldn't feel the same sense of euphoria she was feeling.

"I'm just wondering what would have happened if all this hadn't been thrust on you…"

"All what?" she asked in genuine puzzlement.

"Responsibility for the Legacy. Chad's murder. Me."

"I'm not sure I followed that progression."

"If you and I had met under different circumstances, would we be here now?"

It was a legitimate question. And one she couldn't answer. She hadn't been looking for a relationship, not even when she'd begun this one. And as he'd suggested, it had happened for all the wrong reasons.

"I don't know," she said. "Does it matter?"

"I guess that depends on where we go from here."

"Where we go?" she repeated carefully.

"You eventually heading back to Connecticut, for example."

Only a few days ago that had been something she'd wanted more than anything else. Now it didn't sound the least bit appealing. And the man lying beside her was a large part of the reason for that.

"I'm not leaving until I can be sure the foundation is in good hands. Actually…I'm not entirely convinced that mine aren't the best hands for that. I can't believe I'm saying that, by the way."

"Why not? It's true."

"I'm not sure the board would agree."

"Then they're fools. You're the one who discovered something was wrong."

"Chad did that, but he wasn't as lucky as I've been."

"Lucky?"

"He didn't have you. I don't think I can do this without you," she said.

Only when the words were out of her mouth did she realize how much a plea for help they were. And perhaps a plea for something else. A commitment he might not want to make.

"You won't have to."

"I don't think Cabot is going to be willing to make this a permanent assignment."

"I wasn't talking about an assignment," he said. He bent his head, dropping a kiss on the tip of her nose.

"Then…what were you talking about?"

"Us," he said softly.

Her heart paused and then resumed beating, but at an increased pace. *Us.* She wondered if that could possibly be as promising as it sounded.

"Us?" she echoed.

"I know there are things to consider, but despite our differences…" Again the words faded.

"What differences?"

"I'm a steak-and-potatoes kind of guy, remember. I don't even own a tux."

"That isn't a prerequisite to a relationship," she said, feeling her anxiety ease.

This she could handle. The things he was worried about didn't amount to a hill of beans. Not to her.

"Not even a relationship with Kelly Lockett?"

"You've already got all the important stuff covered. All you have to do is—"

Love me. The words were on the tip of her tongue, and yet she couldn't bring herself to say them. He had given her no indication that he did. She didn't want to put words in his mouth.

After a moment he prodded, "All I have to do…?"

Still she hesitated. He had shown her in a dozen ways that he cared about her. He had risked his life to protect hers.

That was his job, she reminded herself. Maybe she had been reading into those actions more than she should.

"Kelly?"

She refused to meet his eyes, feeling as if she'd made a fool of herself again. On the night she met him, she had invited him into her bed. And now…

"I liked what you said before," she hedged.

"What I said before?"

"Us," she said, finally meeting his eyes. "I like that whole concept."

"The concept, huh?" A thread of amusement lurked in the deep voice.

"Are you making fun of me?"

"Absolutely not. I like the concept, too. I just wasn't sure how I'd fit into your world."

"My world for the past few years has been running an inn in the wilds of nowhere. This…" Her eyes left his to touch on the elegance around them. "This was Chad's world. I'm only occupying it for a short time."

"And you believe there's room in this world for me? Even after Cabot is satisfied this is over."

"Before you came…" she began. Unexpectedly tears stung behind her lids. She forced herself to go on. "Before you came, it was the darkest, emptiest place I'd ever been in my life."

"That's what I'm afraid of."

"That I want you there because of that?"

"Do you?"

"Not gratitude. Not loneliness," she said, pushing up to touch her lips to his. "And not any of the other things you're determined to imagine. I want you here because I *want* you here. With me. I was hoping that's what you wanted, too."

For a long moment he didn't move. Then, as she watched, the corners of his mouth tilted upward. She took a breath, a little shocked at what was in his eyes.

"Part of it," he said. "We'll work the rest out as we go along."

"The rest?"

"The happily-ever-after stuff."

"You believe in that?"

"Don't you?"

She wasn't sure she ever had before. But then she'd never known anyone like him before. "I think I do now."

"Good," he said as if that settled everything.

Maybe it did. Maybe that's all it took. Just believing. And as his lips lowered again to hers, she realized in this case that wasn't going to be a stretch at all.

HARLEQUIN®
INTRIGUE®

has a new lineup of books to keep you on the edge of your seat throughout the winter. So be on the alert for...

BACHELORS AT LARGE

Bold and brash—these men have sworn to serve and protect as officers of the law...and only the most special women can "catch" these good guys!

UNDER HIS PROTECTION
BY AMY J. FETZER
(October 2003)

UNMARKED MAN
BY DARLENE SCALERA
(November 2003)

BOYS IN BLUE
A special 3-in-1 volume with
REBECCA YORK (Ruth Glick writing as Rebecca York),
ANN VOSS PETERSON AND PATRICIA ROSEMOOR
(December 2003)

CONCEALED WEAPON
BY SUSAN PETERSON
(January 2004)

GUARDIAN OF HER HEART
BY LINDA O. JOHNSTON
(February 2004)

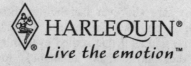

HARLEQUIN®
® *Live the emotion*™

**Visit us at www.eHarlequin.com
and www.tryintrigue.com**

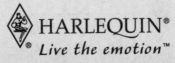

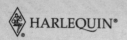

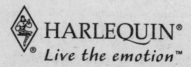

HARLEQUIN *Super*ROMANCE®

Koomera Crossing

**Welcome to Koomera Crossing,
a town hidden deep in the Australian Outback.
Let renowned romance novelist Margaret Way
take you there. Let her introduce you to
the people of Koomera Crossing.
Let her tell you their secrets....**

Watch for

Home to Eden,

**available from Harlequin Superromance
in February 2004.**

And don't miss the other Koomera Crossing books:

Sarah's Baby
(Harlequin Superromance #1111, February 2003)

Runaway Wife
(Harlequin Romance, October 2003)

Outback Bridegroom
(Harlequin Romance, November 2003)

Outback Surrender
(Harlequin Romance, December 2003)

Visit us at www.eHarlequin.com   HSRKOOM